The Haunt⟨ed M⟩ountain

The Famous JUDY BOLTON Mystery Stories

By MARGARET SUTTON

In Order of Publication

A JUDY BOLTON Mystery

The Haunted Fountain

BY
Margaret Sutton

Illustrated by Pelagie Doane

APPLEWOOD BOOKS
Bedford, Massachusetts

The Haunted Fountain
was originally published in 1957.

Reprinted by permission of the estate of Margaret Sutton.
All Rights Reserved.

———————

For a complete list of titles in the Judy Bolton Mysteries,
please visit judybolton.awb.com.

Thank you for purchasing an Applewood Book.
Applewood reprints America's lively classics—books from
the past that are still of interest to modern readers.
For a free copy of our current catalog, write to:

Applewood Books
P.O. Box 365
Bedford, MA 01730
www.awb.com

ISBN 978-1-4290-9048-3

MANUFACTURED IN THE U.S.A.

She was again at the mercy of the foaming spray

A Judy Bolton Mystery

THE HAUNTED
FOUNTAIN

By

Margaret Sutton

Grosset & Dunlap

PUBLISHERS NEW YORK

The Haunted Fountain

TO SALLY
Who Helped Us Explore
A Real Haunted Fountain
Like the One in This Story

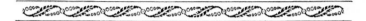

Contents

x   Contents

CHAPTER I

An Unsolved Mystery

"Tell Judy about it," begged Lois. "Please, Lorraine, it can't be as bad as it appears. There isn't anything that Judy can't solve."

Lorraine tilted her head disdainfully. "We're sisters now. We're both Farringdon-Petts and should be loyal to each other. But you always did take Judy's part. She was the one who nearly spoiled our double wedding trying to solve a mystery. I don't believe she'd understand—understand any better than I do. Everyone has problems, and I'm sure Judy is no exception."

"You're right, Lorraine," announced Judy, coming in to serve dessert to the two friends she had invited for lunch at Peter's suggestion. "I do have

1

problems, and there are plenty of mysteries I can't solve."

"Name one," charged Lois. "Just mention one single spooky thing you couldn't explain, and I'll believe you. I've seen you in action, Judy Bolton—"

"Judy Dobbs, remember?"

"Well, you were Judy Bolton when you solved all those mysteries. I met you when the whole valley below the big Roulsville dam was threatened by flood and you solved that—"

"That," declared Judy, "was my brother Horace, not me. He was the hero without even meaning to be. He was the one who rode through town and warned people that the flood was coming. I was off chasing a shadow."

"A vanishing shadow," Lois said with a sigh. "What you did wasn't easy, Judy."

"It didn't need to be as hard as it was," Judy confessed. "I know now that keeping that promise not to talk about the dam was a great big mistake and could have cost lives. I should have told Arthur."

"Please," Lorraine said, a pained expression clouding her pretty face, "let's not talk about him now."

"Very well," Judy agreed. "What shall we talk about?"

"You," Lois said, "and all the mysteries you've solved. Maybe you were mistaken about a thing or two before the flood, but what about the haunted house you moved into? You were the one who tracked down the ghosts in the attic and the cellar and goodness knows where all. You've been chasing ghosts ever since I met you, and not one of them did you fail to explain in some sensible, logical fashion."

"Before I met you," Judy said, thinking back, "there were plenty of them I couldn't explain. There was one I used to call the spirit of the fountain, but what she was or how she spoke to me is more than I know. If my grandparents knew, they weren't telling. And now they're both dead and I can't ask them. They left me a lot of unsolved mysteries along with this house. Maybe I'll find the answers to some of them when I finish sorting Grandma's things. They're stored in one end of the attic."

"Another haunted attic? How thrilling!" exclaimed Lois. "Why don't you have another ghost party and show up the spooks?"

"I didn't say the attic was haunted."

Judy was almost sorry she had mentioned it. She wasn't in the mood for digging up old mysteries, but Lois and Lorraine insisted. It all began, she finally told them, the summer before they met. Horace had just started working on the paper. Judy remembered that it was Lorraine's father, Richard Thornton Lee, who gave him his job with the *Farringdon Daily Herald*. He had turned in some interesting church news, convincing Mr. Lee that he had in him the makings of a good reporter. And so it was that he spent the summer Judy was remembering in Farringdon where the Farringdon-Petts had their turreted mansion, while she had to suffer the heat and loneliness of Dry Brook Hollow.

Her thoughts were what had made it so hard, she confessed now as she reviewed everything that had happened. She just couldn't help resenting the fact that her parents left her every summer while they went off on a vacation by themselves. What did they think she would do?

"You'll have plenty to read," her father had told her. "I bought you six new books in that mystery series you like. When they're finished there are plenty of short stories around. Your grandmother never throws anything away. She has magazines she's saved since your mother was a girl. If you ask for them she'll let you have the whole stack. I know how you love to read."

"I do, Dad, but if the magazines are that old—"

Judy had stopped. She had seen her father's tired eyes and had realized that a busy doctor needed a vacation much more than a schoolgirl who had too little to do. He and Judy's mother usually went to the beach hotel where they had honeymooned. It was a precious memory. Every summer Dr. Bolton and his wife relived it. And every summer Judy went to stay with her grandmother Smeed, who

scolded and fussed and tried to pretend she wasn't
glad to have her.

"You here again?" she had greeted her that summer, and Judy hadn't noticed her old eyes twinkling
behind her glasses. "What do you propose to do with
yourself this time?"

"Read," Judy had told her. "Mom and Dad say
you have a whole stack of old magazines—"

"In the attic. Go up and look them over if you
can stand the heat."

Judy went, not to look over the old magazines so
much as to escape to a place where she could have a
good cry. It was the summer before her fifteenth
birthday. In another year she would have outgrown
her childish resentment of her parents' vacation or
be grown up enough to ask them to let her have a
vacation of her own. In another year she would
be summering among the beautiful Thousand Islands
and solving a mystery to be known as the *Ghost
Parade*.

"A whole parade of ghosts," Lois would be telling
her, "and you solved everything."

But then she didn't even know Lois. She had no
idea so many thrilling adventures awaited her. There
seemed to be nothing—nothing—and so the tears
came and spilled over on one of the magazines. As
Judy wiped it away she noticed that it had fallen
on a picture of a fountain.

"A fountain with tears for water. How strange!" she remembered saying aloud.

Judy had never seen a real fountain. The thrill of walking up to the door of the palatial Farringdon-Pett mansion was still ahead of her. On the lawn a fountain still caught and held rainbows like those she was to see on her honeymoon at Niagara Falls. But all that was in the future. If anyone had told the freckled-faced, pigtailed girl that she would one day marry Peter Dobbs, she would have laughed in their faces.

"That tease!"

For then she knew Peter only as an older boy who used to tease her and call her carrot-top until one day she yelled back at him, "Carrot-tops are green and so are you!"

Peter was to win Judy's heart when he gave her a kitten and suggested the name Blackberry for him. The kitten was now a dignified family cat. But the summer Judy found the picture of a fountain and spilled tears on it she had no kitten. She had nothing, she confessed, not even a friend. It had helped to pretend the fountain in the picture was filled with all the tears lonely girls like herself had ever cried.

"But that would make it enchanted!" she had suddenly exclaimed. "If I could find it I'd wish—"

A step had sounded on the stairs. Judy remembered it distinctly. She had turned to see her grand-

mother and to hear her say in her usual abrupt fashion, "Enchanted fountain, indeed! If you let people
know your wishes instead of muttering them to
yourself, most of them aren't so impossible."

"Were they?" asked Lois.

She and Lorraine had listened to this much of what
Judy was telling them without interruption.

"That's the unsolved mystery," Judy replied.
"There weren't any of them impossible."

And she went on to tell them how, the very next
day, her grandparents had taken her to a fountain
exactly like the one in the picture. It was in the center
of a deep, circular pool with steps leading up to it.
Beside the steps were smaller fountains with the
water spurting from the mouths of stone lions. Judy
had stared at them a moment and then climbed the
steps to the pool.

"Am I dreaming?" she remembered saying aloud.
"Is this beautiful fountain real?"

A voice had answered, although she could see no
one.

"Make your wishes, Judy. Wish wisely. If you
shed a tear in the fountain your wishes will surely
come true."

"A tear?" Judy had asked. "How can I shed a
tear when I'm happy? This is a wonderful place."

"Shed a tear in the fountain and your wishes will
surely come true," the voice had repeated.

"But what is there to cry about?"

"You found plenty to cry about back at your grandmother's house," the mysterious voice had reminded her. "Weren't you crying on my picture up there in the attic?"

"Then you—you *are* the fountain!" Judy remembered exclaiming. "But a fountain doesn't speak. It doesn't have a voice."

"Wish wisely," the voice from the fountain had said in a mysterious whisper.

CHAPTER II

If Wishes Came True

"DID you?" Lois interrupted the story to ask excitedly. "Oh, Judy! Don't keep us in suspense any longer. What did you wish?"

"Patience," Judy said with a smile. "I'm coming to that."

First, she told her friends, she had to think of a wise wish. There had been so much she wanted in those early days before the flood. Dora Scott had been her best friend in Roulsville, but she had moved away.

"You see," she explained, "I made the mistake of having just one best friend. There wasn't anybody in Dry Brook Hollow. I remember thinking of how lonely I was and how I wished for a friend or a sister, and suddenly a tear splashed in the water. It made little ripples. I thought I had to wish quickly before they vanished, and so I began naming the things I wanted as fast as I could. I'm not sure they were wise wishes. They seem rather selfish to me, now. I wasn't thinking of anybody but me, Judy Bolton, and what I wanted. It wasn't until after I began to think of others that my wishes started to come true."

"But what were they?" Lois insisted.

Lorraine seemed unusually quiet and thoughtful. Judy did not notice the fear in her eyes as she replied airily, "Oh, didn't I tell you? I wished for lots of friends and a sister, and I wished I could marry a G-man and solve a lot of mysteries and that's as far as I got when the ripples vanished. I thought the spell was broken and so I didn't wish for anything more."

"Wasn't there anything more you wanted?" Lois asked.

"Of course," replied Judy. "There were lots more things. I wanted to go places, of course, and keep pets, and have a nice home, and—"

"And your wishes all came true!"

"Every one of them," Judy agreed, "even the one about the sister. You see, it wasn't a baby sister I wanted. It was a sister near my own age. That seemed impossible at the time, but the future did hold a sister for me."

"It held one for me, too," Lois said, squeezing Lorraine's hand under the table. "Don't you think sisters should tell each other their problems, Judy?"

"Honey and I always do," she replied "but then it was different. I didn't know I would marry Peter or that he would become a G-man, and he didn't know he had a sister. It is strange, isn't it? But the strangest thing of all was the fountain itself."

"Why?" asked Lorraine. "Do you still think it was enchanted?"

Lois laughed at this, but Judy was serious as she answered, "I was still little girl enough to think so at the time. I wandered around, growing very drowsy. Then I found a hammock and climbed into it. I must have gone to sleep, because I remember waking up and wondering if the voice in the fountain had been a dream."

"A hammock? Lois questioned. "Are you sure it wasn't a flying carpet?"

"No, it was a hammock all right," Judy assured her, laughing. "It was hung between two trees in a beautiful garden all enclosed in rose trellises thick with roses. Did I tell you it was June?"

"All the year around?"

Again Lois laughed. But Lorraine said abruptly, "let's not talk about rose gardens in June. It's a long way from June to December."

"Do you mean a garden changes? I know," Judy

said, "but I think this one would be beautiful at any time of the year. There were rhododendrons, too, and I don't know how many different kinds of evergreens. I explored the garden all around the fountain."

"And then what happened?" Lorraine urged her.

"Yes, yes. Go on," entreated Lois. "I didn't dream you'd kept anything that exciting a secret. Why didn't you try to solve the mystery?"

"I think I would have tried," Judy admitted, "if I had been older or more experienced. I really should have investigated it more thoroughly and learned the secret of the fountain. But after the ripples went away it didn't speak to me any more, and I didn't really think it had heard my wishes. I was still wishing for a friend when I met you, Lois. It did seem impossible for us to be friends at first, didn't it? Lorraine was your friend."

"I did make trouble for you," Lorraine remembered. "It was all because of my foolish jealousy."

"It was nothing compared to the trouble caused by the Roulsville flood," declared Judy. "After that things started happening so fast that I completely forgot about the fountain. Honestly, Lois, I don't believe I thought about it again until after we moved to Farringdon and I walked up to your door and saw the fountain on your lawn."

"The Farringdon-Pett puddle, I always called it,"

Lois said with a giggle. "I've seen lots nicer fountains."

"You have?" asked Judy. "Then maybe you've seen the one I've been telling you about. I think the picture of it is still in the attic. Come on up and I'll show you."

Lois and Lorraine had finished their dessert while Judy was telling them the story of the fountain. Somehow, she wasn't hungry for hers. She had tasted it too often while she was making it.

"I'll leave it for Blackberry," she decided.

Lois watched in amusement as the cat lapped up the chocolate pudding after Judy had mixed it generously with cream.

"Sometimes," Judy said fondly, "Blackberry thinks he's a person. He eats everything we eat, including lettuce. Do you mind if he comes with us, Lorraine? He wants to explore the attic, too."

"He'll remember he's a cat fast enough if there are any mice up there," Lois said with a giggle.

Leaving the table, they all started upstairs with the cat bounding ahead of them. In modernizing her grandparents' house to suit her own and Peter's tastes, Judy had seen to it that the old stair door was removed. But there was still a door closing off the narrower stairs that led to the attic. Blackberry reached it first and yowled for Judy to open it.

"He can read my mind. He always knows where

I'm going," Judy said as the door creaked open and the cat shot through it. A moment later a weird rolling noise came from the floor above.

"Come on. There's nothing up here to be afraid of," Judy urged her friends.

"Maybe not, but I'm beginning to get the shivers," confessed Lois as she followed Judy to the sewing room at the top of the last flight of stairs.

"So am I," Lorraine admitted. "I'm not superstitious about black cats, but they are creepy. Does Blackberry have to roll spools across the floor?"

"Now he thinks he's a kitten," laughed Judy. Pausing at still another door that led to the darker part of the attic, she turned and said mysteriously, "Up here we can all turn back the clock. Does anybody care to explore the past?"

The exploration began enthusiastically with Judy relating still more of what she remembered about the fountain.

"When I told Grandma about it she laughed and said I must have dreamed it. She said if wishes came true that easily she'd be living in a castle. But would she?" Judy wondered. "When I first remember this house she was still burning kerosene lamps like those you see on that high shelf by the window. I think she and Grandpa like the way they lived without any modern conveniences or anything."

"I think so, too," Lois agreed, looking around the

old attic with a shiver. "It is strange they both died the same winter, isn't it?"

"Maybe they wanted it that way. Maybe they wished neither of them would outlive the other. If they did wish in the fountain," Judy went on more thoughtfully, "I'm sure that was one of their wishes. Another could have been to keep the good old days, as Grandma used to call them. That one came true in a way. They did manage to keep a little of the past when they kept all these old things. That's what I meant about turning back the clock."

"If wishes came true I'd like to turn it back a little myself," Lorraine began. "It would be nice if things were the way they used to be when I trusted Arthur—"

"Don't you trust him now?" Judy asked.

Afterwards she was sorry for the interruption. Lois and Judy both questioned Lorraine, but that was all she would say. Judy wondered, as they searched through the old magazines, what was wrong. Lorraine was of a jealous disposition. Was the green-eyed monster coming between her and her handsome husband, Arthur Farringdon-Pett? Until now they had seemed blissfully happy. But there was no happiness in Lorraine's face as she gazed at a picture of one of the fountains and then said in a tight little voice, "It is. It's the very same one."

"But that's the picture I've been searching for!

Judy said eagerly. "Do you know where it is?"

"I can't be sure. But if it ever was enchanted, I'm sure it isn't now. Let's go," Lorraine said suddenly to Lois. Judy knew she was suggesting a fast trip home. But, apparently, Lois did not understand it that way. If she did, she pretended not to.

"Where?" she asked. "To the fountain? I'd love to, wouldn't you, Judy?"

"I certainly would," Judy replied enthusiastically. "Do you recognize it, too?"

"I think so," Lois answered after studying a little more closely the picture they had found. "It looks like the fountain on the Brandt estate."

"The department store Brandts?" Judy questioned. "Then my grandparents must have driven old Fanny all the way to Farringdon."

"Not quite all the way," Lorraine objected. "The Brandts own that stretch of woods just before you come into the city. You've passed it lots of times."

"Of course," agreed Judy. She put the magazine back in its place under the eaves and turned eagerly to her friends. "I do remember a road turning off into the woods and going on uphill," she told them. "I never thought it led to a house, though. There isn't even a gate. Could that be the road my grand-parents took?"

"Why don't we take it ourselves and find out?" Lois suggested.

CHAPTER III

A Strange Encounter

LORRAINE was not too enthusiastic about the proposed trip to the Brandt estate. Finally she agreed to it under one condition. They were not to drive all the way to the house which, she said, was just over the hilltop. They were to park the car where no one would see it and follow the path to the fountain.

"But suppose we can't find the path?" asked Judy.

"You'll remember it, won't you?"

Judy thought she would, but she wasn't too sure. She and Lois both argued that it would be better to inquire at the house. Lois knew Helen Brandt slightly.

"She'd be glad to show us around. This way it looks as if we're planning a crime," Lois said as they started off in the blue car she was driving.

It was a neat little car, not too conspicuous, and easy to park in out-of-the-way places. Judy laughed and said if they did find the fountain she thought she'd wish for one exactly like it.

"Well, you know what your grandmother said about wishes, don't you?" Lorraine asked. "If you let people know about them instead of muttering them to yourself most of them aren't so impossible."

"Quite true," Judy agreed. "I'll let Peter know about this one. He's my Santa Claus, and it will soon be Christmas. Maybe I should have worn the fur coat he gave me last year."

"Your reversible's better in case it rains. It's too warm for snow. We picked a perfect day for this trip," Lois continued, guiding the car around curves as it climbed the steep hill beyond Dry Brook Hollow.

The trip was a short one. In twenty minutes they had covered the distance that had seemed such a long way to Judy when she was riding in her grandfather's wagon.

"I've been thinking about it," she said, "and I've just about figured out how it happened. I didn't think my grandparents knew the Brandts well enough to pay them a visit, though. We must have looked queer driving up to a beautiful estate in Grandpa's old farm wagon. I do remember that Grandma had some hooked rugs to deliver. But that still doesn't explain what happened afterwards. When I woke up in the hammock I was alone in the garden. Horse, wagon, grandparents—all had disappeared."

"How could they?" asked Lois.

"Anyway," Lorraine began, "you had a chance to see how beautiful everything was before—"

Again she broke off as if there were something she wanted to tell but didn't quite dare.

"Before what?" questioned Judy.

"Oh, nothing. Forget I said anything about it. You were telling us how you woke up in the hammock, but you never did explain how you got back home," Lorraine reminded her.

"Didn't I?" asked Judy. "I'd forgotten a lot of it, but it's beginning to come back now. I do remember driving home along this road. You see, I thought my grandparents had left me in the garden for a surprise and would return for me. I told you I was all alone. There wasn't a house in sight."

"The Brandt house is just over the top of this next hill," Lois put in.

"I know. You told me that. Now I know why I couldn't see it. All I could see was a windowless old tower and a path leading in that direction. Naturally, I followed it. There's something about a path in the woods that always tempts me."

"We know that, Judy. Honey told us all about your latest mystery. You followed a trail or something."

"Well, this trail led out of the rose garden where the hammock was and then through an archway," Judy continued. "All sorts of little cupids and gnomes peered out at me from unexpected places. I was actually scared by the time I reached the old tower. There wasn't time to explore it. Just then I heard the rumble of my grandfather's wagon and knew he was driving off without me."

"He was!" Judy's friends both chorused in surprise, and Lois asked, "Why would he do a thing like that?"

"I think now it was just to tease me. He did stop and wait for me after a while," Judy remembered. "The rugs were gone. Grandma must have delivered them, but I didn't ask where. If she made them for Mrs. Brandt they may still be there."

"I wouldn't depend on it," Lorraine said as they turned up the narrow road to the Brandt estate.

"Watch out!" Judy suddenly exclaimed. "There's another car coming."

As Lois swerved to avoid the oncoming car, Lorraine ducked her head. She kept herself hidden behind Judy until the car had passed. The man driving it was a stranger to Judy, but she would remember his hypnotic, dark eyes and swarthy complexion for a long time. The soft brown hat he was wearing covered most of his hair.

"What's the matter with you two?" asked Lois when the car had passed. "Aren't you a little old for playing hide and seek?"

"I wasn't—playing. Let's not go up there," Lorraine begged. "I don't think the Brandts live there any more."

"Maybe not, but we can pretend we think they do, can't we?" Judy replied a little uncertainly.

She was beginning to suspect that Lorraine knew more about the Brandt estate than she was telling.

Lois kept on driving along the narrow, gravelly road. Soon there were more evergreens and a hedge of rhododendrons to be seen. They looked very green next to the leafless trees in the woods beyond. The sky was gray with white clouds being driven across it by the wind.

"There's the tower!" Lorraine exclaimed. "I can see it over to the left. It looks like something out of Grimm's Fairy Tales, doesn't it?"

"It looks grim all right," agreed Judy. "I wonder what it is."

"I suppose it's nothing but an old water tower. It would be fun to explore it, though," Lois said. "But if there are new people living here they'll never give us permission."

"We might explore it without permission," Judy

suggested daringly. "Come on!" she urged her friends as Lois parked the car in a cleared place beside the road. "Who's going to stop us? And who wants to explore a gloomy old tower, anyway? Let's look for the fountain."

"Do you think we should?" Lorraine asked. "It won't be enchanted. I told you—"

"You told us very little," Lois reminded her. "If you know anything about the people who live here now, I think you ought to let us know. Otherwise, I'm afraid we won't be very welcome."

"I don't think they'll welcome us, anyway. I do know who they are," Lorraine admitted. "You remember Roger Banning from school, don't you? I've seen him around here. His family must have acquired sudden wealth, or else he's just working on the estate."

"Then you've been here lately? Why didn't you tell me?" asked Lois. "We always used to go places together."

"It wasn't important," Lorraine replied evasively. "I was just out for a drive."

"You plutocrats!" laughed Judy. "Each with a car of your own. You're not interested in Roger Banning, are you, Lois? I'm sure you can do better than that. I did know him slightly, but not from school. The boys and girls were separated and went to different high schools by the time we moved to

Farringdon. I remember his pal, Dick Hartwell, a lot better. He was in our young people's group at church."

"Sh!" Lois cautioned her. "Nice people no longer mention Dick Hartwell's name. He's doing time."

"For what?" asked Judy.

Like Peter, her FBI husband, she preferred facts to gossip.

"Forgery, I guess. He stole some checkbooks from his father's desk and forged the names of a lot of important business people. I think he forged some legal documents, too. Anyway, he went to the Federal Penitentiary. It was all in the papers," Lorraine told her.

Now Judy did remember. It was something she would have preferred to forget. She liked to think she was a good judge of character, and she had taken Dick Hartwell for a quiet, refined boy who would never stoop to crime.

"I don't see what all this has to do with the fountain," Lois said impatiently. "Are we going to look for it, or aren't we?"

"Of course we are. That's what we came for. I just like to know what a tiger looks like before he springs at me," Judy explained.

"You seem to think there's danger in this expedition of ours, don't you?" asked Lorraine.

"I don't know what to think. You're the one who seems to know the answers, but you're not telling.

Hiding your face back there gave you away. You've seen that character who drove down this road and, for some reason, you were afraid he would see you. Why, Lorraine? Why didn't you want to be recognized?"

Lorraine hesitated a moment and then replied evasively, "People don't generally enter private estates without an invitation. That's all."

"I'd better turn the car around," Lois decided, "in case we have to leave in a hurry. I don't expect we'll encounter any tigers, but we may be accused of trespassing."

"I'm sure we will be," announced Judy as two dark-coated figures strode down the road toward them. "You drove right by a NO TRESPASSING sign, and this isn't a welcoming committee coming to meet us!"

CHAPTER IV

Unwelcome Visitors

"OH DEAR! I wasn't quite quick enough," Lois complained as she gave the steering wheel another turn.

Judy and Lorraine had gotten out of the car to direct her as she turned the car around. Now it refused to budge, spattering mud as the wheels spun. The two men came nearer, shouting and waving their arms.

All at once Judy recognized one of them as Roger Banning. His light hair emphasized the angry flush that covered his face.

"What are you girls doing here?" he demanded. "Can't you read?"

"Oh dear! I wasn't quick enough."

Lois had an answer for that. She spoke fearlessly in spite of her predicament.

"You should know, Roger. You went to school with us. I should think you'd help instead of yelling at us. One little push on the back of the car ought to do it. Please!"

"Go ahead, help her," the huskier man said.

With that Roger and the other man almost lifted the car back on the road where it was soon turned in the other direction. Lois smiled sweetly as she thanked them.

"Are you friends of the Brandts?" she asked.

"That's not the point," Roger Banning retorted. "You and your girl friends are trespassing on private property."

"I can explain why we came here if you'll listen," Judy put in quietly. "When we started on this trip we thought the Brandts still lived here. Lois knows Helen Brandt from school. We thought she'd be glad to show us around the estate."

"You did, eh? Well, nobody gets shown around this estate. Now get going!"

"Wait a minute. Don't hurry us." Judy's voice was still quiet. "What, exactly, is your objection to showing people around?"

"It ain't a showplace," the other man objected.

"It was when the Brandts lived here. We didn't know they'd sold the estate."

"They haven't," was the reply. "They went to Florida for the winter and leased it to us. Why don't you drop in for a call after they get back?"

"Watch it, Cubby," Roger Banning warned him. "I wouldn't be handing out any invitations if I were you. I recognize this girl now. She's Judy Bolton, or was, before she married that smart young lawyer, Peter Dobbs. Her brother's that pasty-faced newspaper reporter they call the hero of the Roulsville flood. Dr. Bolton's on the staff at Farringdon Hospital and that's where these kids will wind up if you let—"

"Watch it yourself," the heavy-set young man called Cubby interrupted.

They both glared at her, waiting for her to explain herself further. But what could she say? Her wide gray eyes must have told them she was baffled.

Lorraine was not saying a word. As she shielded her face with her hands she looked like a poor, frightened bird trying to hide under its own wing.

"She's really in trouble," thought Judy, "and these men know something about it."

Determined to find out something herself, she faced them unflinchingly. It was Lois who finally apologized for the intrusion, explaining that she had been a guest of the Brandts several times and felt sure they wouldn't mind if she and her friends had just one more look at the fountain.

"Fountain! What fountain?" Roger Banning laughed derisively. "There's no fountain on the estate and never has been. You girls have taken the wrong road if you're looking for a fountain."

"I don't think we have," Lois told him calmly.

"What about the tower?" asked Judy. "We noticed what looks like a water tower over there in the woods. Isn't it used to store water for the fountain?"

"It is no longer in use. Now will you leave?"

"I think we'd better," Lorraine whispered, pulling Judy toward the car.

It seemed the only thing to do. The two young men who had made up what Judy called the "unwelcoming committee" watched them as they drove off down the road. When they were nearly to the main highway Lois laughed and said, "If they think they've scared us away they're greatly mistaken. I'll hide the car the way Lorraine suggested. It wasn't such a bad idea after all."

Judy helped her find a secluded place just beyond the entrance to the estate. Apparently people had picnicked there in the summertime. A big evergreen tree with branches dipping to the ground hid the car from view while the girls planned their next strategy.

"We'll find that fountain if it's the last thing we do," declared Judy. "The idea of telling us it doesn't exist! You girls both saw it, didn't you?"

"That—that was years ago," Lorraine said. "They —they could have torn it down or something."

"I don't believe they did. We just drove past the path without seeing it," Lois declared.

"It will be easier to find if we walk back. Let's do it," Judy suggested. "We should have walked up to the estate in the first place. Then they wouldn't have heard us coming."

"But suppose they see us?" Lorraine objected, holding back.

"They won't bite—if you mean those two over-grown schoolboys," Judy said. "Anyway, I don't believe they have any more right on the estate than we have. They weren't necessarily telling the truth about it. Do you know the other one, Lois?"

"Cubby? No, I'm afraid I don't."

"What about the third character, the one who passed us in the car?"

"I never saw him before," declared Lois. "Did you, Lorraine?"

Her silence was answer enough. She had seen him before, but she was afraid to say so. If he lived on the estate, Judy decided it might be a good idea for them to do their exploring before he returned.

"I wouldn't care to have him catch us, would you?" she questioned.

Lorraine finally agreed to Judy's plan, and they started back up the narrow road. They had not walked far when they came to the sign that Lois had chosen to ignore the first time.

NO TRESPASSING, it warned them in big black letters. ALL PERSONS ARE FORBIDDEN TO ENTER THESE PREMISES UNDER PENALTY OF THE LAW.

"We can't walk right past it," Lorraine objected as they stopped to read the sign.

"I don't see why not. We drove right past it," Lois returned with a defiant toss of her head. "Who cares about their old sign, anyway? I'm sure the Brandts wouldn't forbid us to come here. They may even thank us for it."

These puzzling words only partially convinced Lorraine. But Judy was beginning to enjoy the adventure. She studied the NO TRESPASSING sign a moment more and then began to laugh.

"It says ALL PERSONS," she told her friends as they walked deliberately past it, searching for the path to the fountain. "Who *is* permitted to enter, I wonder—ghosts?"

"Spirits, maybe, like the one that spoke to you," Lois said with a shiver.

"Then the fountain wouldn't be enchanted at all. It would be *haunted*," declared Lorraine.

And suddenly she held back, afraid.

CHAPTER V

Forbidden Ground

"Come on, Lorraine," urged Lois. "We were only joking. You know there's really no such thing as a haunted fountain. And perhaps they really have torn it down."

"I haven't been here since that day I came with my grandparents, but we won't find out by just standing here," declared Judy. "I think those men had some reason for telling us the fountain didn't exist, and I mean to find out what it was. I should have brought Blackberry along. He was my excuse for exploring the ruined castle. I was supposed to be looking for my cat."

"What did you do with him?" Lois questioned.

"Blackberry?" Judy gave a little gasp. "I am careless! I do believe I left him shut in the attic, but Peter will rescue him when he comes home."

"We may need him to rescue us if those men find out what we're up to. What time do you expect him?" Lorraine wanted to know.

"He said he might be late and suggested that I spend the night with Mother and Dad," replied Judy. "I didn't ask him why. You know Peter doesn't want me to get myself involved in any of his cases. I don't even know what sort of assignments he has any more. The Bureau is so secret about it."

"Well, we can be secret about this investigation, too. How do we know those men aren't criminals hiding out here while the Brandts are away?" asked Lois.

"Roger Banning isn't a criminal," Lorraine objected.

"His pal, Dick Hartwell, was. Remember?"

"Wasn't there something in the paper about him being out on parole?" asked Lorraine. "I don't think we should label him a criminal if he is. Probably he has a good job and is no more inclined toward crime than we are. After all, we are trespassing."

"I don't care if we are," Lois said recklessly as they trudged on.

It seemed a long way uphill to the part of the estate where Judy felt sure the path branched off and led toward the fountain.

"Watch for it! We don't want to miss it. Maybe we ought to look for it on the other side of that hedge," she suggested.

"How can we?" asked Lois.

"We'll go back to where the hedge begins," declared Judy. "It's the only way."

"We'll be all afternoon finding it," complained Lorraine. "Maybe the fountain isn't haunted, but it is creepy here in the woods. You know, Judy, I've missed most of your shivery adventures. I wouldn't be so interested in this one if it didn't directly concern me."

Judy didn't see how, but she was curious. She waited until they were well concealed behind the hedge. It was safer, just in case someone did drive up the road. Then she turned to Lorraine and said as casually as she could, "That's so. Lois did say you had a problem. What is it, Lorraine? Don't you want to tell me about it?"

Apparently she didn't. Nobody spoke for a minute. Then Lois said, "She won't even tell me. I just know something is wrong from the way she acts."

"I didn't say anything was," Lorraine protested.

"You did say something about not being able to trust Arthur," Judy reminded her. "Do you still want to turn back the clock so that things will be the way they were before you quarreled?"

"We didn't quarrel," Lorraine retorted quickly.

"Maybe you should," Judy began. "Peter and I do occasionally. Dad says it's good for us. He says it clears the air, and we do love each other all the more after we make up. If you'd tell Arthur about this problem—"

"Please," Lorraine stopped her. "Can't you see the way it is? If I could tell him or anyone else about it, then it wouldn't be a problem. I just want to believe in things the way I did when I was a little girl. I mean impossible things like wishes coming true."

"But they do come true if you work at it. Mine did," Judy reassured her.

Lorraine started to say something more, but broke off suddenly as Lois stumbled into what she felt sure must be the path.

"You were right, Judy!" she cried excitedly. "They've concealed it on purpose. We couldn't possibly have seen it from the road. There isn't a break in the hedge."

The path didn't look very much as Judy remembered it, but she agreed that it might not have been used recently.

"Anyway," she said, "it's going in the right direction. We should pass the tower and then come to a rock garden with statues—what's this?"

A fence with barbed wire running from post to post was directly across the path.

"Shall we crawl under it?" asked Lois.

"We might climb over it," Judy suggested. "The wires seem loose. I'll hold them down."

"Wait! They're electric!"

The warning from Lois came just too late. Without noticing the white insulators attached to it, Judy had put her hand on the top wire. Quickly she drew back with a sharp cry of pain.

"Don't touch those wires!" she warned Lorraine. "I guess they mean that sign back there. This fence is charged with electricity. It gave me quite a shock."

"I burned my hand—almost," Lois corrected herself as she looked and saw no burn. "It felt like it, but I guess those wires aren't really deadly."

"I *hope* not." Lorraine turned to Judy and asked a little plaintively, "What do we do now?"

"I have an idea," Judy replied, looking around for a forked stick. When she had found one of just the right size she was able to hold back the wires without receiving any more electric shocks. As soon as Lois and Lorraine had crawled under the fence, she gave them the stick to hold for her.

"Now," she announced, standing erect and brushing herself off, "we're really on forbidden ground."

All three girls followed the path beyond the fence. White statues, like white ghosts, loomed up in unexpected places. Over to the left was the tower. Lois glanced at it and then shivered.

"It gives me the creeps," she confessed. "Do you

think somebody could be up there watching us?"

"I don't see how," replied Judy. "The tower has no windows."

"There may be a stairway inside. Look!" Lois suddenly exclaimed. "There's a broken statue."

It was a cupid-like figure with the head broken off at the neck. Judy didn't see it until Lois pointed it out. There it lay beside the marble base that had once supported it. A little farther along the path its head grinned up from a thicket. Lorraine saw it first and uttered a piercing scream.

"Sh!" Judy warned her. "You don't want Roger Banning and his heavyweight friend to follow us, do you? It's only a piece of that broken statue."

"I know. I guess I'm nervous," Lorraine confessed.

"There's no need to be," Lois put in. "You can see this part of the estate is deserted. Lots of old showplaces like this are going to pieces. We may find they were telling the truth about there not being any fountain. People just don't go to the expense of keeping up these big estates."

Judy didn't think this was true of the Brandts. Everyone knew Mr. Brandt had made millions with his chain of department stores. He might employ a caretaker for the estate in his absence, but she didn't really think he would lease it.

"Except, of course, to friends," she added.

"The Bannings could have been friends. It's *their*

friends who worry me," Lorraine admitted.

"That one we met in the car when you hid your face?" Lois questioned. "You were afraid of him. I could see that."

"I just didn't want him to recognize me," Lorraine said, and quickly changed the subject.

They had reached the rose trellis, now bare of roses. It, too, had been broken. A bird bath Judy remembered leaned at an angle. She found a tree with a hook in the trunk and cried out excitedly, "This is the hook that held one end of the hammock. Now I know exactly how I walked to reach the fountain. I should think you could hear it from here. I did then."

She stood for a moment listening and then walked on, growing more puzzled by the minute. Lois and Lorraine followed. It was a strange walk. Everything was familiar and yet oddly different. Not a sound could be heard except the crunch of their own footsteps along the path toward the fountain.

"Where is it?" Lorraine whispered. "It was here."

"Yes, it was," agreed Lois, "but that was in the summer. It's winter now. Maybe they turned it off for fear the pipes would freeze or something."

"That must be it. I can see the circle of cement," announced Judy. "There should be steps going up to it. We can explore what used to be the fountain. We may find a clue to my old mystery!"

CHAPTER VI

A Diamond Clue

"A CLUE, did you say? Now we're looking for clues," Lois said with a laugh as she followed Judy toward what they now felt almost sure was the broken and deserted fountain.

"It's a shame, isn't it?" asked Judy. "It used to be so beautiful."

"You remember it in the summer," Lois reminded her again. "Now it's winter. Things naturally change with the changing seasons."

"Not this much," Judy objected. "It isn't the same at all. There should be steps—"

"There are!" Lois interrupted.

Lorraine found them and almost bumped into one

of the stone lions beside them. He seemed to have a startled expression on his face.

"You should have said, 'Excuse me, Mr. Lion!' " Lois teased her.

"This is the fountain all right," declared Judy. "Those stone lions used to have water spurting out of their mouths. Now there's nothing but a rusty old water pipe."

"So that's what gives Mr. Lion such a startled expression?" Lois cocked her head to one side and made a face at the statue.

"Is that Mrs. Lion on the other side?" asked Judy. "They look exactly alike. There should be eight of them guarding the four flights of steps leading up to the pool. I remember running up and down those steps and meeting all the lions. Shall we do it again?"

"Let's!" cried Lois, seizing Judy's hand.

"Wait!" urged Lorraine. "Stop acting like children. I think there's still a little water in the main fountain, and if there is, I intend to make my wish."

"So *we're* acting like children?"

Lois looked at Judy and giggled, but Lorraine was serious. She walked sedately up the steps to the circular pool and peered over the edge.

"You can't wish," Judy called, "unless you shed a tear. The spirit said so."

"The spirit is gone, and so is most of the water," declared Lois.

"All the better for exploring. I would like to see what's over there. Do you think I can make it?" asked Judy.

"You can try," Lois told her. "We'll follow you if you don't get your feet wet."

"I won't. I wore my rubbers. Anyway, there's a thin coating of ice over what little water there is left in the pool. I'll just skate over to the center fountain and have a look."

It was not quite as easy as it sounded. Judy had some difficulty climbing over the edge of the pool and sliding down into its nearly dry bottom. The ice turned out to be nothing but melting slush from an earlier snowfall. She waded through it to the smaller circle of cement immediately surrounding the pedestal which was ornamented with cupids. At their feet she found a pool that had not been drained. A cap that looked like the nozzle of a watering pot covered another rusty waterpipe that seemed to be clogged with dead leaves. Judy peered into a cave behind the cupids, trying to see what was there.

"What have you found?" called Lois, seeing something in Judy's hand.

"A sprinkler, I guess. There's a cave that seems to go down underneath the fountain. I can't see anything in it but rusty pipes. Could the spirit voice have come from there?"

"It seems logical, doesn't it?"

"You sound like Peter," laughed Judy. "There's nothing logical about a spirit that lives in a fountain. I'm a little disappointed that it's all so ordinary, now. Maybe we shouldn't have come."

"Let's go then," Lorraine suggested. "I can't wish if there isn't any water—"

"There is a little. I don't know why it wouldn't work just as well, especially if you shed a tear."

"I can't turn my tears on and off like a faucet," Lorraine objected. "Couldn't we throw in a coin or something?"

"People toss coins in wishing wells. Shall we try it?" asked Lois.

"Come on over and try it if you think it will do any good," Judy invited them.

"It does seem a shame to throw perfectly good money away. Would a penny do?" Lois asked after she had helped Lorraine across. "I suppose you have to feel enchanted."

"I did." Judy stopped and listened. "Do you hear anything? Maybe the voice will still speak to us if we're perfectly quiet."

"Out of a dry fountain? Oh, Judy!" Lorraine cried. "I did so want to wish. It's the only thing left to do."

"Why?" asked Lois.

"That's what everybody keeps asking," Lorraine replied in a rush of sudden emotion. "Why? Why?

And I keep asking myself the same question. Maybe it was silly of me to think I could wish away a problem as serious as this, but I have to do something. I can't go on like this, holding it all back and pretending—"

"Then don't hold it back. Tell us, dear!" Judy urged her.

"Oh, if only I could! If only I could cry my heart out and tell you everything!" sobbed Lorraine.

And suddenly, as she leaned over the little pool that was left around the fountain she did shed a tear that splashed in the water and made ripples all around the spot where it fell.

"Wish! Wish!" Judy and Lois cried both together.

They were so excited that they heard only part of what Lorraine whispered into the fountain.

". . . it wasn't Arthur," the wish ended and then, as the ripples vanished, Lorraine sobbed, "Oh, but it was! It was! How can I keep on loving him if I can't trust him? Judy, could you love Peter if—if you thought he was a—a *cheat?* Could you?"

"I wouldn't think it—even with proof. I mean it," declared Judy. "I've learned my lesson. Once I did doubt him, and then when I found out what was really happening I was so ashamed. No matter what happened now, I'd keep on trusting him because I love him, and loving him because I trust him. The two go together—"

"It looks—like a diamond!" gasped Judy

Suddenly Judy stopped speaking. She had been idly dabbling her hand in the pool as she talked. Now she felt something small and hard at the bottom. "Like a small gravel stone," she thought as she took it between her thumb and forefinger to examine it.

"Have you found another clue?" asked Lois. "What is it this time?"

"It looks—like a diamond!" gasped Judy. "But it can't be. What would a diamond be doing in an old deserted fountain?"

"It could be a piece of ice," Lorraine ventured.

"A frozen tear, perhaps," Lois put in whimsically. "Maybe the tear you shed, Lorraine, turned into a diamond. Maybe there are more diamonds in the pool. Maybe we'll walk home with our hands full—"

"We'll walk home dripping wet if we aren't careful! The fountain is beginning to bubble!" cried Lorraine as she seized her friend's hand and pulled her away from the water. Judy stood spellbound watching the transformation as if a miracle had taken place. Finally Lois expressed the obvious.

"Someone has turned it on!"

"Someone in the tower," guessed Judy.

"Or down underneath," Lorraine whispered. "Judy, I'm scared. This was planned, somehow. I think we're being watched!"

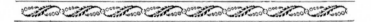

CHAPTER VII

A Moaning Cry

"THIS is a real diamond," declared Judy.

She brought her find over to the edge of the pool to examine it more closely. Then she turned to gaze in wonder at the fountain.

Soon it was not only bubbling. It was sending great sprays of water in all directions—from the center of the high pedestal, from the cupid-like creatures that held it, over the cave behind them and from the mouths of the eight stone lions that guarded the four flights of steps going down from the fountain.

"It's beautiful!" breathed Judy. Then, in a louder voice, she called to her friends, who were huddled together over by the yew hedge. "See how fast the pool is filling up! Now the little pool where I found the diamond has vanished and everything looks just the way I remember it. Even the cupids look alive now that they're all wet and shiny."

"It's haunted with all sorts of queer noises," cried Lorraine. "Don't stand so close to it, Judy. You may get wet."

"I wouldn't mind," she replied, still under the spell of the fountain.

A little of the spray had wet her coat and covered her hair with a mist that made it cling to her forehead in damp, red ringlets. She brushed them back with a laugh and turned again to listen.

"I'm all right. This warm coat protects me," she began.

"From the water, yes! But are any of us protected from those men back there?" asked Lois.

"We've been seen. I know we have!" Lorraine's voice was almost hysterical. "Somebody saw us and turned on the fountain full force!"

"Look at the way it sparkles and dances as if it were filled with diamonds!" Judy exclaimed. "You two girls may be used to fountains, but I'm not. This one does something to me."

"Me, too," Lorraine said with a shiver. "It scares me. Come on away from it, Judy. We ought to be going home."

Judy, still reluctant to leave, walked around the fountain to where they were. As she came nearer

Lois said, "Look at your hand, Judy! You didn't lose the diamond out of your engagement ring, did you? That could be the diamond you found in the fountain."

Judy checked quickly, but the diamond in her ring was intact. She had lost it once, but that was another mystery. Now the new prongs held it securely. It was about the size of the stone she had found. Comparing the two as well as she could in the fading daylight, Judy now felt certain of her discovery.

"This is a clue to something," she declared, tying the diamond she had found in the corner of her handkerchief for safekeeping. "You girls weren't wearing diamonds, were you?"

"I wasn't," Lois replied.

"My ring isn't a diamond. It's a ruby," Lorraine began and then broke off abruptly, hiding her hand.

"But you aren't wearing it!" Judy exclaimed. "Where is that gorgeous big ruby Arthur gave you, Lorraine? I've never seen you without it before."

"Neither have I. What have you done with it?" asked Lois. "You haven't lost it, have you?"

"I guess—I must have," Lorraine explained lamely.

"Where? In the fountain? Then we'll hunt for it," declared Judy.

"I'm sure it isn't in the fountain," Lorraine said hurriedly. "Besides, it's growing dark. If we don't leave now we won't be able to find the path."

"But we can't go without your ring," Lois protested.

"Of course not," agreed Judy. "Where do you think you lost it?"

"Maybe it *was* in the fountain? Oh dear!" Lois lamented. "Now the water is on we won't be able to look for it. That fountain must attract jewels—"

"Or tears," Lorraine said, "but it doesn't matter. We wouldn't find it there, anyway."

"Why wouldn't we? Do you know where you lost it?"

"Did you take it off?"

"Was it loose on your finger?"

Judy and Lois were both firing questions at Lorraine. They were questions that she seemed unable to answer. Finally she admitted that she had removed the ring from her finger on purpose.

"Why?" demanded Lois. "I don't think that was fair to Arthur."

"I don't either," agreed Judy.

"But I did it for him," Lorraine protested.

"You did what? Took off your ring? Why?" asked Judy. "How could that help him?"

"I can't tell you," Lorraine said stiffly. "Please don't ask me anything more about it. We've all behaved like children today—me with my wishes and you with your pretending. If that is a diamond you found, Judy, it's no frozen tear."

"I know," Judy admitted. "It belongs to someone, I suppose, and we'll have to report it. I remember how I felt when my diamond was lost. Someone else may be feeling the same way."

"If we report it," Lois said, "we'll have to report the fact that we were trespassing. I'd rather find out who lost it some other way."

"We could advertise." Judy brightened at the thought. "We could tell Horace—"

"And have him spread our little adventure all over the front page of the paper. Oh, no, you don't," Lorraine objected. "I've seen what happened to other stories you told your brother. Besides, I don't want my father to know. He's editor, and he'll look into any story that has my name in it."

"I didn't think of that," Judy admitted. "What I can't understand, Lorraine, is why you took off your ring—"

"Look," Lorraine interrupted, "can't we just forget it? My ring is gone. It's been gone for several days if you must know. I'll get it back somehow."

"How?" asked Judy.

"Wishing, maybe. I don't know how else."

"Do you mean someone's stolen it?"

"I didn't say that."

"No, but you implied it."

Judy soon discovered her questions were leading her nowhere. It was all very confusing. The diamond

she had found and the ring Lorraine had lost seemed
to be clues to something, but she couldn't figure out
what.

"Maybe the fountain will tell us where it is," Judy
was beginning with a laugh when suddenly they all
heard a low moan. It seemed to come directly from
the fountain.

"Wh-hat was that?" gasped Lois.

Lorraine had turned pale.

"Sh!" Judy cautioned them.

If the fountain had anything to say, she wanted to
hear it. A chill came over her as she waited. Lois
and Lorraine huddled together, shivering. The moan
came a second time and with it the long drawn-out
words, "Go-oo a-wa-ay!"

"He doesn't need to tell me twice. I'm going!"
declared Lois. "Come on, Judy! Why are you standing there?"

"I'm not afraid of a voice. If someone is trying to
scare us, he will have to think of something more
frightening than that. I'm just puzzled. Before, it was
a woman—or a girl."

"What was?" asked Lois and Lorraine both together.

"The voice from the fountain. It wasn't a man, and
it wasn't moaning. There it is again!"

Thoroughly frightened, Lois and Lorraine rushed
ahead of Judy down the path. It was already so dark

they had difficulty following it, but the moans that were following them gave wings to their feet. Only Judy was reluctant to leave. She turned to the fountain, as if it were alive, and called, "I'll be back! I will, too," she reiterated, catching up with her two friends, who were determined to leave with or without her. "I'll be back first thing in the morning, and either Horace or Peter or both of them will be with me. I'm not going to let any moaning fountain keep me from finding out what's going on."

Lorraine stopped short. They had come to the fence. Now a voice shouted at them from another direction.

"Who's there? Stop where you are!"

"He's back!" exclaimed Lorraine, panic-stricken. "That's the man who passed us in the car! We mustn't let him stop us!"

"We won't," promised Judy, "but I'm afraid we'll have to stop long enough to protect ourselves from these electric wires. Here's the stick I used before. I'll hold them back while you girls crawl under them."

Lois and Lorraine quickly obeyed. But they did not wait for Judy. Stumbling, falling, picking themselves up and hurrying on, they were out of sight while she was still struggling to get through the fence.

CHAPTER VIII

Judy Is Warned

"HAVING trouble?" a sneering voice inquired.

Judy had managed to prop up the wires and slide under them by herself without receiving a shock. She was about to hurry on when the dark man Lorraine feared approached her. It was not hard to pretend that she, too, had been frightened.

"I—I'm all right now. I—just want to get out of here," she chattered. "That fountain back there must be haunted. I heard moans coming from it."

"Is that all you heard?"

"That was enough!" declared Judy, not admitting to any curiosity concerning the moans. "I just want to go—"

"Go, then, and don't come back!" the man

warned. "We don't want strangers snooping around here."

Judy was thankful he thought she was a stranger. Apparently he hadn't seen Lois and Lorraine. As she hurried on, Judy kept telling herself that they wouldn't leave without her. And yet, when she finally reached the spot where they had parked the car Lois was in the very act of driving away.

"Wait!" shouted Judy. "What kind of friends are you to leave me here after I helped you through the fence? How did you think I would get home?"

"We didn't think. Oh, Judy! I'm sorry," Lois apologized. "Are we being followed?"

"No, I don't think so. He went back up the hill, but not before I had a good look at him. He's just a man. No horns! He warned me not to come back."

"You won't, will you?"

"I'm considering—"

"There isn't time to consider now. Hop in, Judy," Lorraine commanded, "if you don't want us to drive off without you. It would serve you just right for getting us into this."

Judy hopped in, but she wasn't happy about leaving. She didn't like running away from a mystery.

"I got you into it?" she asked when they were on their way. "From the way you've been acting, Lorraine, you were in serious trouble before I mentioned the fountain, and I suspect that man back there has something to do with it. I was only trying to help—"

"Well, don't try any more. It's no use."

"Maybe not," agreed Judy, and changed the subject. "It gets dark so quickly, these December evenings," she observed. "But it's still early. See? The lights are still on in the stores," she added as they drove into Farringdon.

She had planned to spend the night with her mother and go Christmas shopping with her early in the morning. Now she was rapidly changing her plans to include Horace.

"Let me off at the newspaper office," she said to Lois when they reached Main and Grove Streets. "Horace may be working late. I don't care what you girls say, I have to at least put a notice about this diamond in the Lost and Found column."

"I suppose you do," Lois agreed. "Knowing you, I'm sure you wouldn't keep it without advertising for the owner."

"Do you have to mention where you found it?" Lorraine asked anxiously.

"No, but I do have to go back there. Suppose we're needed? That moan sounded as if the—the fountain hurt somewhere—"

"How could a fountain hurt?" asked Lois.

"The same way it could speak, I suppose. If I knew, I wouldn't be so eager to explore it. As for your problem, Lorraine," Judy finished as Lois stopped the car to let her out, "I think it will solve itself if you just trust Arthur and put his ring back on your finger."

"I would if I could," Lorraine said sadly. "Good-bye, Judy. We both wish you luck."

"I'll need it," thought Judy as she headed for the *Herald* Building just opposite the county courthouse where Peter worked. The resident agency of the FBI would be located in the new Post Office as soon as it was completed. The Ace Builders, Arthur's company, was in charge of construction.

Judy entered the front office where she received permission to hunt up Horace somewhere in back. Finally she found him pecking away at his typewriter and looking immensely dissatisfied with what he had written.

"Hi, sis!" he greeted Judy. "Why so gloomy? You look better in a smile."

"Thanks, brother of mine," replied Judy, smiling at him. "I was thinking gloomy thoughts, I guess. For a girl whose wishes come true, I ought to know better. Horace, I have something to tell you."

"I surmised as much. Well, let's have it!"

Quickly she told him the story of the fountain, adding the information that their grandparents had been friends of the Brandts.

"That's where they must have taken you all right," he agreed, "but what of it? Why should

something that happened five or six years ago worry
you now?"

"It doesn't—not any more. It's something that
happened today."

Horace grinned expectantly.

"Let's have it then. It's time for all honest people
to stop working, but newspapermen never stop.
Things have a way of happening at night. Is what
you have to tell me news, by any chance?"

"Not yet," she replied, "but I think I'm on the
trail of something that will be. I only hope it doesn't
happen at night, because I want to go there with you
tomorrow morning."

"Where?" he asked. "Not to that enchanted fountain you were telling me about? That's for kids. It
has to be some place important if I go on the newspaper's time. Not only that, I have to give a reason
for going."

Judy told him several good reasons, adding that
she had been warned to stay away by a mysterious
character who seemed to frighten Lorraine.

"He knows Roger Banning and a heavy-set friend
of his called Cubby," she continued. "They apparently live there. They say the Brandts leased the estate to them, but I don't believe it. They said there
wasn't any fountain, but we found not only a fountain but a diamond in the water. As Lorraine says, it's
no frozen tear. Take a look at it, Horace!" Judy un-

tied her handkerchief and exhibited the gem. "There!" she finished. "Now is it important? Do you think we should advertise?"

"Not yet. Jeepers, what a piece of ice! Think we can find any more of them scattered around that fountain?"

"We can try. Please go with me," begged Judy. "You'll have to think of some excuse—"

"Tell you what," Horace decided. "I won't use this story I have in the typewriter. It's supposed to be a writeup for my 'Meet Your Neighbor' column, but now I have another neighbor in mind. This week the readers of the *Farringdon Daily Herald* will meet George Banning, father of Roger. He used to be a plumber, but he must have some more lucrative job now if he can afford to lease the Brandt estate. I'll just assume he's somebody important. Think that will get us in?"

Judy smiled. "I think so. A plumber might be employed by the Brandts to repair the fountain, but that doesn't make sense, either, does it? The fountain was still badly in need of repair."

On the way home Judy told Horace more about the mysterious fountain and the moaning cry she had heard.

"Are you sure it wasn't just a noise in the pipes?" Horace asked dubiously.

"It wouldn't say 'Go away!' would it?"

"You might have thought it did. The air would come out with a peculiar sound if someone suddenly turned on the water."

That, in Horace's opinion, could account for the "voice" in the fountain. He expounded his theory later around the dinner table. It had holes in it, as Judy soon pointed out to her parents. Dr. Bolton was especially interested in the moan.

"Someone could be in pain. You say you didn't have time to explore underneath the fountain?"

"We couldn't, Dad, with the water turned on. I think there is a place to go down behind those cupids that hold the pedestal, but the water shoots right over it. Lorraine acted as if she thought that man she seems so afraid of was trying to drown us. She and Lois almost drove off without me."

"That was unkind of them," Mrs. Bolton began in the overly sympathetic tone she sometimes used.

"Oh, Mother! You just don't understand them," Judy objected. "They knew each other long before they met me. Besides, we're—well, different. We don't care about being proper the way a Farringdon-Pett does. Roger Banning did say a funny thing, though. It was something about Dr. Bolton's kids winding up as the patients if Cubby would let them. That wasn't just the way he said it. Dad, what do you think he meant?"

"I don't know," the doctor admitted, "but I'll be

at the hospital between eleven and twelve o'clock. Call me there if you need me. Perhaps you'd better call anyway," he added. "I'm a little worried about this haunted fountain, as you call it. I haven't forgotten the haunted road. Your ghosts very often need medical care."

"I see what you mean, Dad."

Judy had not forgotten the haunted road, either, or her terrifying experience at the end of it. Now she was deep in a new mystery. The spirit of the fountain had not called for help, she reminded her father. The voice had called, "Go away!" She was sure of that.

"Probably it was only one of those boys hiding under the fountain and trying to frighten you," Mrs. Bolton said. "They might have known they would only whet your curiosity. Have you told Peter about it?"

"I haven't seen him," replied Judy. "Has he called?"

Judy's mother said he hadn't. "Perhaps you'd better call him," she added. "Tell him there's a nice chicken pie I can warm up for him if he hasn't had dinner."

"I think he has, Mother. From the way he spoke I think he had plans for the whole evening. But I'll call, anyway."

Judy dialed the number and soon heard the telephone ringing in her own house in Dry Brook Hollow. It was right beside the door so that she could hurry in and answer it if she happened to be outside. Peter had another outside wire in his den, and there was an extension in their bedroom. Nobody could complain that it took too long to reach the telephone. After six rings Judy decided there was nobody at home.

"Peter may be on his way here. If he is, I hope he let Blackberry out of prison. I think I shut him in the attic by mistake," confessed Judy. "He was up there playing with my sewing things."

"Thinks he's a kitten, does he?" chuckled the doctor. "I wouldn't worry about him if I were you, Judy girl. Cats have a way of taking care of themselves."

"Blackberry does. Peter will think the house is haunted if he comes in and hears him rolling spools around up there. He will investigate the noise, and Blackberry will be rescued—like that!" Judy finished and dismissed the matter from her mind.

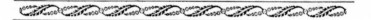

CHAPTER IX

Horace Cooperates

JUDY really meant to call Peter again. But when his sister Honey telephoned and suggested a late movie she couldn't resist the temptation to go with her. The picture was all about a man with a criminal record. It made Judy think of Dick Hartwell. Honey said she had liked him, too.

"My trouble is, I like everybody," she confessed. "Besides, I have a little theory of my own that people have to make mistakes in order to do better. I know I did."

"I believe in that, too," declared Judy, "and so does Peter. He doesn't think a single conviction should brand a man as a criminal. I certainly had a better opinion of Dick Hartwell than I do of Roger

Banning. He and that Cubby, as he calls him, are up to no good. As for that other man, there was something evil about him. Lois and Lorraine weren't the only ones who were frightened. I do mean to go back there and investigate in spite of his warning. Horace will dig up something. I wish you could go with us tomorrow, Honey. You couldn't ask for the day off, could you?"

"I'm afraid I couldn't," Peter's sister replied. "Mr. Dean has just bought a new air-brush machine, and tomorrow is the day I learn how to use it. I wouldn't miss that even for a wish in your enchanted fountain, Judy. The art work I'm doing is the fulfillment of my dearest wish, anyway. But have fun!"

"I will," Judy promised, wondering if she would.

The next morning when Judy told Horace what Honey had said about the new air-brush machine, he was not pleased at all. Muttering that young Forrest Dean was more interested in the artists his father employed than in the work he was supposed to be doing, Horace made an attack on his breakfast that sent a fried egg skimming through the air like a flying saucer.

"Ha! Ha! Ha!" screeched his parrot from his cage near the kitchen window.

Fortunately for the doctor's peace of mind, the parrot went to sleep early, but he also awoke at the crack of dawn. This morning he was especially noisy.

"At least," Judy laughed, as Horace mopped up the egg, "he isn't calling names the way he usually does."

"No?" asked Horace.

The egg incident had started the parrot off. Now he was sidling from one end of his perch to the other and screeching, "Cheat! Cheat! Cheat!"

This was by no means the only word in the parrot's vocabulary, but it was the one he most frequently used. It made Judy think of Lorraine's wish.

"She wished she could trust Arthur, and then she asked me if I could trust Peter if I believed he was a cheat. What do you think she meant by that?"

"Cheat! Cheat!" shrieked the parrot.

"There! You've started him off again. Quiet, Plato!" commanded Horace.

To Judy's amazement, the bird kept still.

"So you've finally decided on a name for him?" she asked her brother. "But why Plato?"

"Why not?" Horace asked. "Most of his chattering is Greek to me. Honey suggested the name. You know how I feel about her, Judy. But if she's in love with her art work, where do I fit in?"

"I'm afraid, Horace, that she thinks of you as a brother," Judy told him. "After all, she is my sister. I wished for her in the fountain, and my wish came true."

"Actually," Horace pointed out, "she is your sister-in-law, but it doesn't matter. I'll be a great big cooperative brother to both of you if that's the way she wants it. Art before love, as the saying goes. By the way," he asked more curiously, "how does Honey operate this air-brush machine?"

"She doesn't know," Judy replied. "That's why she's so eager to learn. She told me the kind of picture it paints. It gives a nice spattered effect like—like the spray from a fountain."

Everything reminded her of fountains. Later, as they drove through Farringdon and on toward the Brandt estate, they talked of little else.

"We'll see what haunts your fountain, and then I'll take you on home. This may not be much of a story, sis. I hope you won't be disappointed."

"I won't be. I'm more interested in what's bothering Lorraine. Something has made her really unhappy," Judy declared. "You and I both know Arthur wouldn't do anything dishonest. Why should Lorraine, who's supposed to be in love with him, even suggest that he might be a cheat?"

"Did she?" Horace looked almost too interested.

"I started to tell you at breakfast, but your parrot wouldn't let me. Maybe I shouldn't have mentioned it. Lorraine acts as if the whole thing ought to be kept secret, and I'm sure she has a reason. Horace—"

"Don't worry," he assured Judy. "I won't let the cat out of the bag."

Again Judy thought of Blackberry shut in the attic.

"Maybe we should drive over to my house—"

"Later," Horace promised, turning in at the private road to the Brandt estate. "Newspapermen never pay any attention to NO TRESPASSING signs," he told Judy as they drove past the notice and straight up to the door of the house Judy was now seeing for the first time.

The top of the hill had looked like the end of the world. They had come down upon the house immediately afterwards. It was nestled in the hollow beyond the hilltop and rambled off in all directions, an attractive combination of brick and native stone. There were three or four tall chimneys. Judy didn't count them because, just as she and Horace climbed out of the car, a black cat darted in front of them and through the open door. A grim, elderly man, who did not look at all pleased to see them, was holding it open. He had not waited for Horace to ring the bell.

"*Herald* reporter. May I have an interview?" Judy's brother asked promptly.

"With whom, may I ask?"

The man's tone was icy, but Horace replied in his usual bland manner, "I was told by my editor to get a good story from someone of importance. I leave it to you, sir. Who is the most important person here?"

The man, who was tall, white-haired, and rather

an important-looking person himself, was about to reply when a woman's voice from somewhere within the house called, "Who is it, Stanley?"

"Reporters, madam," replied Stanley, raising his voice as much as dignity would permit. "They want to interview a person of importance. Will you see them?"

"I will not." The reply was short and to the point. "I told those two gentlemen who were here last night that we have nothing to hide. I will not be bothered by any more people."

Horace, who always had a quotation at the tip of his tongue, turned to Judy and said, " 'The lady doth protest too much, methinks.' "

"I beg your pardon?" Stanley said politely.

It came to Judy that he must be the butler. Had the Brandts left him there to take care of things while they were away, or had these new people, whoever they were, hired him? Even the Farringdon-Petts didn't employ a butler.

"This is the residence of Mr. and Mrs. Banning, isn't it?" she asked.

"Brandt," Stanley corrected her. "I'm afraid you have made a mistake—"

"I'm afraid *you* have made a mistake," Horace said, and his tone was not so bland as before. "The Brandts are in Florida. We were told they had leased the estate to the Bannings. Is Mr. George Banning here?"

"He is not, sir!"

"What about his son, Roger?"

"He isn't here, either. Stanley, tell them to go away!" the voice from upstairs called more shrilly. "Roger is out. He won't be back until afternoon."

"We'll wait, if you don't mind. We're in no hurry."

Pushing himself past the startled Stanley, Horace pulled Judy along with him. "There's news here," he whispered, "and I don't mean small stuff. Unless my eyes deceive me, that's a police car driving up the road. We can watch from this window!"

CHAPTER X

Blackberry Leads the Way

THE room in which Judy found herself seemed to be all windows. There was no furniture in it except for a round rug on the polished floor and a bench against one wall. In the other three walls were high windows with deep cabinets built under the window sills. On top of them were big glass tanks and little glass tanks filled with everything from tiny tropical fish to goldfish the size of flounders. Horace nearly dived into one of the fish tanks as he rushed to look out and see what was happening. Nothing, apparently, was.

"They're simply cruising around out there," he observed. "Do you think they're looking for the fountain?"

"They won't reach it in a police car," Judy replied. "They—" She stopped suddenly. The round rug on the floor was hand-hooked and looked very familiar. So was the cat that sat motionless in the center of it, fascinated by the moving fish.

"Horace!" she exclaimed. "That's Grandma's rug! She did deliver it here, and that looks like—it is!" Gathering the cat in her arms with another exclamation, she hugged him against her cheek and then, holding him back to look at him, asked in amazement, "Blackberry! What in the world are you doing here?"

"What he intended to do was obvious," Horace observed with a grin. "What would any cat do in a room full of fish? I didn't recognize him when he crossed our path out there and then darted through the door."

"He led us here!" cried Judy. "He's always leading me into adventure."

"And trouble," Horace added. "By the way, sis, are you sure he is Blackberry?"

"Of course I'm sure," replied Judy, tilting the cat's head to show her brother the proof. "No other black cat has the same tiny white hairs that look as if someone had spilled milk on his nose. They're on his feet, too. When I first saw him I said they made him look like a blackberry dipped in sugar, and Peter agreed that Blackberry was a perfect name for him."

"A 'purrfect' name?"

"Exactly," Judy agreed, "with the accent on the *purr*. The white hairs don't show as much as they did when he was a kitten, but I'd know him anyway by the crackle in his purr. Listen to him, Horace! He's so glad to see us."

"I wonder," Horace said, still grinning. "He seemed rather glad to see the fish before we came in. My big news story may turn out to be nothing but a fish story after all. At least I know what his hobby is."

"Whose hobby?" asked Judy. "You don't even know who owns the fish. Stanley could be taking care of them for the Brandts. It does seem to me I remember goldfish in the pool around the fountain."

"When you fished for the diamond you showed me?"

"No, Horace, it was the other time, when I thought the fountain was enchanted and made my wishes. I know I saw flashes of gold in the water. I wonder if any of these fish are ever kept there."

"Probably—in the summer. In the winter the pool seems to be reserved for more valuable things. I wouldn't mind fishing for diamonds. There may be more—"

"Sh!" Judy stopped him. "Wasn't that the door-bell?"

Horace looked out the window. The two policemen who had been cruising around the grounds were no longer in the police car. It was parked in the circular driveway. The bell rang again. Blackberry stiffened in Judy's arms and pricked up his ears. She could hear Stanley's voice.

"Mrs. Cubberling is resting. She does not wish to be disturbed this morning."

"Is she Cubby's wife or his mother?" Judy whispered.

"Who knows? Mr. Cubberling may be the neighbor I'm looking for," declared Horace. "Listen!"

"Two government men were here last night," Stanley was saying. "Mrs. Cubberling can't tell you any more than she told them."

Judy's gray eyes widened in alarm when she heard this. The FBI! Had she accidentally stumbled into a mystery Peter was investigating?

"I didn't mean to!" she exclaimed. "Oh, Horace! One of those government men could have been Peter. What'll we do? I promised him I'd never follow him on another one of his investigations."

"You didn't follow him on purpose," Horace reassured her. "I'm not so sure Blackberry didn't, though. Cats aren't bound by promises."

"I wish girls weren't. I do so want to help—"

"Listen!" Horace interrupted.

The voices outside were becoming louder. Judy heard Roger Banning's name and the name of Dick

Hartwell. Cubby wasn't mentioned. Neither was the dark stranger whose name Judy did not know. Finally Stanley called upstairs in an extremely agitated manner, "There are two gentlemen here, madam. They're officers of the law and they have a search warrant—"

"That does it!" Horace whispered. "It'll be news all right. They're going to search the house."

"They'll find us!" cried Judy. "Horace, they mustn't! That door over there seems to lead to the garden. Maybe we can slip out without being seen."

"An excellent idea! That's using the brain cells. Now," Horace announced a few minutes later when they were safe beyond a thick yew hedge that bordered the garden, "we'll do a little searching for ourselves. Think you and Blackberry can lead me to the fountain?"

"I think so." Judy still had the cat in her arms. "Stop squirming," she told him. "I'll let you down when we find the path."

"Maybe he can help us find it," Horace suggested.

"It wouldn't be safe," Judy objected. "How do we know that dark man isn't lurking around somewhere waiting to catnap him? Seriously, there may be danger. If you come to a fence, don't touch it. The wires are charged with electricity."

"Friendly lot, aren't they?" asked Horace. "There's your fence."

They had come upon it sooner than they anticipated. The whole wooded portion of the estate seemed to be fenced off with chain-link fences and electrically charged wire.

"What do they keep in here?" was Horace's next question. "I'm not eager to meet any ferocious animals."

"The only animals I saw were made of stone," Judy told him. "Lions, but they don't bite. They only spurt water out of their mouths when the fountain is on, and I imagine it isn't today. It's too cold. The pipes would freeze—"

"And moan," Horace said. "You know what weird sounds can come out of hollow pipes when the wind is blowing. You probably only imagined the words."

"I don't imagine words. You know that. Please don't start that argument all over again," begged Judy. "It doesn't get us anywhere, but the path will. This fence crosses it, but I think I can find the place where we got through it yesterday. After that we just followed the path. We can find it all right with the tower to guide us. It's somewhere in that direction."

Judy tried to point, but found the cat in her arms something of a handicap. He was still struggling to free himself.

"You won't hold him long," Horace prophesied.

"But I have to," Judy insisted. "I don't want him to run away from us. He may be a big help if we explore the fountain. If there really is a cave underneath it and if we can squeeze inside, we're bound to find something if only more water pipes. If I can crawl in behind those cupids—"

"*If* the water is turned off," Horace finished for her. "That makes six *ifs*. I counted them."

"There are apt to be seven or eight, if not more," declared Judy. "But Blackberry can explore places we can't. The trouble is, he can't tell us what he finds—"

"Me-aurr!" interrupted the cat.

"In words, I mean," Judy corrected herself. "You tell us in your own way, don't you, Blackberry? I wish you could tell us how you got here. Did Peter bring you?"

"Peter wouldn't bring a cat to help him investigate a crime," Horace began. "Maybe you didn't shut Blackberry in the attic—"

"Blackberry!" cried Judy as the cat leaped from her arms.

It was a squirrel that had attracted him. He soon chased it up a tree and out on an overhanging branch. The squirrel escaped, but Blackberry was now on the other side of the fence. With one leap, he was on the ground.

"A good idea!" approved Horace. "Blackberry is

leading the way again. That's how we'll get over. You're next, Judy. I'll hold you up."

"It seems to me we're doing it the hard way. Oh, my goodness!" she exclaimed when she was in the tree. "I can see the house from here. Those policemen are just coming out. Do you think they'll recognize your car?"

"Probably," replied Horace. He was having a little more difficulty climbing the tree since there was no one to boost him.

"Do you think they'll search the grounds?"

Judy, who was wearing slacks, slid down the branch easily and dropped to the ground, but it broke with Horace. He got up, rubbed a skinned place on his elbow, and replied, "Probably," as if nothing had happened. His dignity seemed to be more hurt than any other part of him. Judy just had to giggle. Blackberry, apparently not liking the commotion caused by Horace's fall, darted off into the bushes.

"He got away in spite of me," declared Judy, "but he'll be back. He likes to help me explore. I would have taken him with us yesterday, but Lorraine doesn't like cats. She says they're creepy."

"She said quite a few unpleasant things, didn't she?" asked Horace.

"It was only because she was upset," Judy excused her. She was beginning to wonder if she should have told her brother anything about Lorraine's problem.

There seemed to be problems enough without that. The next one they encountered was a thick growth of thorny bushes. They were nearer the tower now. The path couldn't be far away.

"If only they hadn't planted so many kinds of holly, and all with prickly leaves," Judy complained. "Maybe they think they need more than electric fences to keep people away."

"Away from what?" asked Horace stopping to extract a thorn from his finger.

"The fountain, I guess. There is some secret about it. There must be," Judy decided. "There! I can see it now, through the bushes, and it is turned off. Hurry, Horace! I can hardly wait to explore it."

CHAPTER XI

Under the Fountain

Judy reached the fountain ahead of Horace. It looked even more forsaken than it had the day before. When they finally stood together beside the circular wall that enclosed the dry pool, even Judy could feel no enchantment.

"It's gone—whatever it was," she said mournfully.

"The water's gone. I can see that much. They must have a good drainage system," Horace commented.

"For the big pool, yes." Judy could not shake off the feeling of disappointment. "There may be a little water in the center fountain," she added more hopefully. "Shall we go across?"

"Might as well," Horace agreed, following her.

Blackberry, who had reappeared, remained at the edge of the pool watching. There were no fish. Thus the fountain held no charms for him.

"Come here, Horace!" Judy called presently to her brother. "You said you wanted to fish for diamonds. Well, this is the place."

Horace found the little pool in the center of the fountain very uninteresting and said so. There was nothing in the water but sticks and dead leaves. Furthermore, it was icy cold.

"Now I understand your frozen tear story a little better," Horace continued. "I suspect Lorraine has more to cry about than she told you. If she doesn't trust Arthur, she has a reason—"

"Perhaps an imagined one. She is jealous. You remember how hard she made it for me in high school —and afterwards. Of course," Judy admitted, "Arthur did like me, and I thought I was in love with him. He is romantic-looking and I was too young to realize that true love is more than going places with someone who makes a nice impression. Peter makes a nice impression, too. But not a romantic one. You sort of feel his strength. Oh, Horace! I wish I'd told him about this before we came. I should have called him instead of going to that movie with Honey."

"I'm afraid we won't find out much, anyway. You say the fountain spoke to you—"

"Yes, but not until I'd made my wish. Yesterday

it was only a moaning sound. I did think it said, 'Go away!' but maybe you were right, Horace. Maybe it was just a noise in the pipes. I'd feel a little foolish speaking to it now."

"More foolish than usual?" Horace teased.

"Just for that I will! Oh, fountain!" Judy began. "Speak—"

A noise in the holly thicket interrupted her. A policeman poked his head through the bushes and shouted, "Hey! What are you doing here?"

"We're just exploring," Judy replied calmly. "If we find anything we'll let you know."

"Oh, it's you," the policeman said and withdrew to go into conference with his companion. Judy heard something in a low voice about previous mysteries she had solved.

"Chief Kelly says he'll never forget the day he met Judy Bolton," she heard. "After emptying a bag of jewels on his desk, she invited him to a ghost party. He tells me she's been chasing ghosts ever since."

"Think that's what *we're* doing?"

"It looks that way. Let Judy and her brother explore the woods if they want to. They're better at finding jewels than we are. There were none in the safe. Mrs. Cubberling was only too glad to have us look there. Who knows? Maybe they'll turn up in a hollow tree."

"Did you hear that?" Judy whispered. "They're

"Hey! What are you doing here?"

looking for jewels. They think maybe we can find them because we did find the loot from that other robbery. Listen!"

There was more conversation as the voices drifted away. Peter's name wasn't mentioned but, because the policemen seemed to approve of what Judy was doing, she felt sure Peter would, too.

"We're trespassing," she told Horace a little later, "but the law doesn't mind. I heard them say they'd made a mistake, but did they? They didn't do much searching around this fountain."

"If there's a story here, we'll just have to uncover it ourselves," declared Horace. "I'd like to explore that tower over there. If there are stairs inside, we could climb them. We'd have quite a view from those peepholes."

Judy saw the peepholes he meant. They were about halfway up the tower. She suspected the police had already viewed the estate from up there and found nothing suspicious. She had not told them about the diamond she had found in the fountain, nor did she intend to tell them until after she had talked the whole matter over with Peter. Apparently only Stanley, the butler, and Mrs. Cubberling had been at home when the house was searched.

"Cubby is probably her husband," Judy decided. It had been a fairly young voice that had called from upstairs. "But where does Roger Banning fit in?" she asked Horace. "Do you think he could be here as a plumber's helper? His father is supposed to be a plumber."

"There are plenty of pipes here. Someone must have to keep them in working order. They've even got them in the lions' mouths."

Judy giggled. "Lois noticed them before. She said it gave Mr. and Mrs. Lion a startled expression, as if they were saying, 'Oh!' "

"Maybe they've found the jewels those policemen are looking for," Horace suggested with a laugh. "Apparently Cubby, as you call him, and Roger Banning made themselves scarce on purpose—"

"And that other man, whoever he was," Judy put in. "He really frightened Lorraine. Did I tell you she lost the ring Arthur gave her? I mean she lost it unless it was stolen. She didn't want to tell us about it, but when we found the diamond I looked to see if it came out of my ring, and then I noticed Lorraine wasn't wearing hers. She acted guilty about it, too. Oh dear! she suddenly exclaimed. "Is that the police car driving away?"

"Sounds like it," agreed Horace. "I felt safer with them here, didn't you?"

"Oh, I feel safe enough," Judy replied carelessly. "Blackberry will protect us. He's up there on the wall keeping watch—"

"Of what?" asked Horace. "Birds?"

"Of course not," retorted Judy. "I trained him not to catch them."

"What about fish?"

There was a twinkle in Horace's eye as he asked this question. He had not forgotten the room with the fish tanks. How Blackberry happened to be there was still a mystery. The house, as well as the grounds, puzzled Judy.

"Something is going on here. Something—fishy." She laughed and then shivered. There was a chill about the deserted fountain that made her wish she had worn warmer clothing. Her hands were especially cold.

"If it's news," Horace said, "it's being well kept from us. Shall we explore below?"

"Let's," agreed Judy. "It can't be any colder down there than it is up here, and I am curious. Come on, Blackberry!" she called to her cat. "Don't you want to help us explore?"

"It's too damp for him," explained Horace when the cat refused to come.

Together Horace and Judy edged in between the cupids. Judy giggled at the pipes running up their backs to the bowl of the fountain. Exploring underneath, they found a dark opening which Horace bravely entered.

"No dragons," he announced, peering about with the help of his flashlight. "It's wet and slippery down here, and there are holes where a person could break a leg. Watch it, Judy!"

The warning came just too late. Judy tripped on something that turned out to be a removable drain cover and fell into what seemed to be a tunnel.

"This would make a good hideout for a gang of thieves," commented Horace when he had helped Judy to her feet. "I hope we're not getting into something we can't handle. Shall we proceed?"

"Of course." Judy was determinedly cheerful in spite of a scraped elbow. "There's nothing dangerous down here."

Horace was not so sure. Cautiously, he led the way along the tunnel, which seemed to be leading directly under the fountain. Suddenly, in the circle of light from Horace's flash, they saw a closed door.

"Maybe this is where Mr. Banning lives!" exclaimed Judy. "Wouldn't it be exciting to live right under a fountain? He could really take care of the pipes—I mean if he is a plumber. It's locked," she added, trying the door. "Shall I knock?"

"What's the use?" asked Horace. "Nobody would answer."

"I'm not so sure of that," declared Judy, rapping loudly on the door.

"I told you," Horace began, but stopped suddenly as the same moaning voice Judy had heard before called out, "Please, go away!"

CHAPTER XII

A Mysterious Prisoner

"THAT," announced Judy when she could find her voice, "was not a noise in the pipes. Someone's in there, and I think he's hurt. Shall I try again?"

Horace did not answer. He stood there as white as a ghost, with his mouth half open. The beam of his flashlight was directed upward. Judy saw a great many water pipes interlaced overhead. She supposed they could carry sound as well as water. But someone had to be in the room to make the sound, and she had a feeling it was someone who needed help and needed it badly. She rapped again, and this time there was no answer.

"Do you need help?" called Judy.

She didn't know this man. She had no idea who he

was. But, being Judy, she was ready to be a friend to anyone in trouble.

"Please answer me! I'm your friend," she called again.

She had to call a third time before the man answered. His voice was fainter now.

"I have no friends," he replied. "Why can't you just go away and let me die in peace?"

For a moment Judy didn't know what to say. She was ready to help him. But how could she?

"He wants to die," she whispered. "Oh, Horace! We must do something. Do you think he's a prisoner in there? Maybe he can't open the door."

"Ask him," Horace suggested.

"Are you locked in?" called Judy. "We'll get you out, somehow, if you are."

"It's no use," the man replied. "I'd rather die here than in prison. Now go away!"

"I think we'd better. We'll have a look around and then notify Peter. This is news, all right," declared Horace. "Probably this man is one of a gang. Maybe he was hurt escaping from the police."

"But Horace," Judy objected, "this man's hurt, and he needs help. We should call Dad."

"Maybe we should. Tell him we'll bring a doctor."

Judy told him, but "Leave me alone!" was the only answer.

"Who are you?" called Horace.

To this and more questions both he and Judy asked there was no answer. The man was through talking and told them so by silence. The air became heavy and oppressive as they waited. From time to time they would call more questions or offer help only to hear their own echoes sounding hollow in the tunnel. There was, Judy noticed presently, one other sound.

"Hear it!" she whispered. "Let's find out what it is. It sounds like someone breathing."

"Maybe it's a dragon breathing fire." Horace was trying to be funny to keep up his spirits. "I'm not feeling like St. George this morning."

"You are a hero," Judy reminded him. "It was in all the papers. 'Hero of the Roulsville flood—' "

"Cut it out, sis! You know I was scared silly. I'm not wearing my suit of armor." Judy knew he was remembering another equally shivery adventure in a ruined castle. "I could use it, though," he added. "Now what are we up against?"

"It looks like another pipe," replied Judy, turning on her own flashlight to see it better. "There's a brick wall beyond it. But what's beyond that?"

Led on by curiosity, Judy soon discovered another locked door. No moans came from behind it, and when she knocked and called there was no answer. There wasn't a sound except—

Judy turned quickly. The sound now came from a

definite direction. Was it something burning? The air was suddenly warm against her face.

"Hey, sis! You know what?" Horace said in a whisper. "There's heat down here, and I don't like it. What do you suppose makes it so warm?"

"It could be only a furnace," Judy said.

She came upon it so unexpectedly that she let out a little shriek and then laughed at herself for doing so. She had been right.

"It is!" she exclaimed. "Oh, Horace! That's all it is. I don't know what I thought it was at first, but it's a little pot-bellied stove with pipes branching out in all directions. Come and see!"

Horace came at once and saw the furnace. There it sat like a squat, red-eyed demon in a little lair of its own. It was burning coal from a bin beside it, and the fire showed through a grate in the door. Horace opened it to show Judy the blaze.

"Comforting, isn't it?" she said. "Though I wonder how they get the coal down here. And who shovels it? I hope, whoever it is, he doesn't shovel us in."

"He might. How do we know he doesn't have horns and a tail? This place needs more than heat to take the chill out of it," Horace said with a shiver. "A little warm sunlight would help."

"There is a little light where we dropped into the tunnel," Judy remembered. "There may be other openings, too. A coal chute, maybe. There must be light of some kind in those locked rooms."

"I hope there is," agreed Horace. "It would be pretty dismal in there where that man is without any light at all."

"He could live down here, I suppose, with light and heat," Judy went on thinking aloud. "But why? Surely nobody would choose to live underground like a mole. If he's hurt, Horace, why doesn't he want us to help him? He said he wanted us to leave him alone to die. It doesn't make sense."

"It does to me," declared Horace. "Obviously, someone has imprisoned him under the fountain for a reason. Maybe he thinks we're his captors and that's why he doesn't trust us."

"But I told him we were his friends," Judy protested.

"But are we? How friendly can we be if he's a criminal?"

"Oh, Horace! He's a human being," cried Judy. "No matter what he's done, he has a right to decent care. We must get him out of there and call Dad or else notify Peter—"

"And have him send the man back to prison?"

"I suppose he'd have to, wouldn't he? If he's an escaped prisoner, or if he's being held here by criminals, Peter may be looking for him. The police weren't. They were looking for jewels. You don't think they're hidden in the room with him, do you?

Maybe he is a thief. Maybe he was hurt trying to escape from the police—or Peter." This thought alarmed Judy. "You know, Horace," she went on more urgently, "he does have to shoot at people sometimes. To make them halt, I mean, If he wounded this man—but he couldn't have done it! It isn't like Peter at all. Oh dear! I'm all mixed up. If I help this prisoner escape I won't be helping Peter, will I? Why do I get into these dreadful situations?"

"It's your instinct to help people," Horace told her with what sounded like real sympathy. "I know how you feel about that man in there, but what can we do if he won't cooperate?"

"We can keep trying," replied Judy. "No matter who he is, we can't leave him in there to die. I'll call him again. Not you, Horace! He might think you were a policeman or something. We can't even let him know you're a reporter. The thought of publicity might scare him, and there's enough down here to terrify him as it is."

"You're not just talking," Horace agreed as they moved closer to the locked door.

"Oh, mister!" Judy called out sweetly. "We're still here, and we still want to help you if you'll let us. We may be strangers, but we want to be friends—"

"Yeah?" The voice behind the door was less polite.

"I know. Friends like Roger Banning—ready to jump on a guy when he's already down."

A friend? Roger Banning? That rang a bell in Judy's mind, but for a moment the thought that followed didn't register.

"Who are you?" she asked. "Do I know you from somewhere?"

"You might tell me who *you* are before I do any more talking," the man replied.

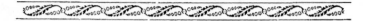

CHAPTER XIII

A Desperate Situation

Judy and Horace looked at each other in bewilderment. They both knew they couldn't tell the prisoner who they were without further antagonizing him. A newspaper reporter and the wife of an FBI agent were hardly the right people to trust with whatever secret the fountain was hiding. Suddenly an idea came to Judy.

"The main thing right now is that you need help," she called out. "If you're hurt we can have Dr. Bolton here in no time. How far is it to the nearest telephone?"

"Too far," the man replied. "I know you now. You're Dr. Bolton's daughter. Is that your husband with you?"

"N-no," Judy stammered, really confused now. "It's my brother."

"The newspaper reporter? Well, why don't you hurry back to your paper and tell them you've rounded up the last of Vine Thompson's boys single-handed? Or didn't you know the Brandts had leased their estate to a gang of jewel thieves? Go ahead, tell them—" Suddenly the excitement died out of the man's voice and he finished in despair. "But it's too late to tell them anything. There's no help for it now. They'll have to send me back to prison."

"What is the story?" asked Horace. "Maybe we can help."

"No, it's no use."

Judy pulled her brother aside where the man wouldn't hear her whisper, "Horace, I know who he is now. He said Roger Banning was a false friend, and he's been in prison, so he must be Dick Hartwell. Don't you see? If he knows us, then we must know him. That's who he is. I'm sure of it. No wonder he's afraid they'll send him back to prison. But he forged some checks. He wasn't a jewel thief. And what did he mean about the last of Vine Thompson's boys?"

"They were jewel thieves. Remember the stolen jewels I found in the hollow tree that used to lean over our house? But of course you remember! You were the one who took them to the police station

and met Chief Kelly and solved most of the mystery—"

"No, Horace," Judy objected. "You solved most
of it. You knew what was haunting our attic long
before I did. I thought maybe it really was Vine
Thompson's ghost."

"If her ghost is anywhere, it's here with the gang
her sons started. I didn't think Dick Hartwell was
in it, though, and it's news to hear that Roger Banning is a jewel thief. Do you suppose that explains
the diamond in the fountain?"

"Sh!" Judy cautioned him. In his excitement,
Horace had spoken louder than he intended. It was
all very confusing. Judy had supposed the Thompson
gang was past history. The sons of the notorious
fence, Vine Thompson, had all received long sen-
tences in prison. But a gang like that, as Peter had
once pointed out to her, spread its evil influence far
and wide. Always there was a criminal on the fringe
of it who didn't get caught. That criminal usually
followed the pattern of his hero, the original gang
leader. And so crime spread, like a bad weed in a
garden. That was the way Peter explained it. How
Judy wished he were here to explain things now!

"Horace," she said suddenly, "you can't breathe a
word of this story until we've talked it over with
Peter and his office has released it. If that man is
Dick Hartwell, he was in a Federal penitentiary. He

forged his father's signature to a government bond."

"But he was out on parole," Horace began.

"He's right, though," Judy interrupted. "They'll put him right back in if they find him. A man is on parole only as long as he keeps out of trouble, and this man is in trouble—way in. I still feel sorry for him, but I know now what we have to do."

"Name it and we'll do it. Of course you'll notify Peter—"

A rushing sound in the pipes overhead interrupted Horace in the middle of what he was saying. His face went suddenly white.

"He heard us!" cried Judy. "I think that man in there heard what we were saying and turned on the fountain!"

"Come on," Horace exclaimed. "We have to get out of here fast, before the fountain fills, and report what he told us. Come on, Judy! The exit must be in this direction. There's that drain cover you tripped on before."

Judy beamed her flashlight toward it and saw that Horace had replaced it.

"Wait!" she called to him. "That drain is there to keep the tunnel from being flooded. If any water seeps in from the fountain it probably runs off down that drain. You shouldn't have put back the cover!"

"I was afraid someone would fall down the hole. Either way, it's a trap!"

Horace's voice sounded hollow, echoing back through the tunnel. Already he was way ahead of her. Judy soon caught up with him, but they were too late. The rushing sound in the pipes overhead continued as the water flowed through them to spray out in all directions from the fountain. Judy couldn't see out. But, remembering, she knew what it must be like out there where she had felt the enchantment.

"Lift me up, Horace," she begged. "You can do it. I want to see."

He lifted her until she could step from his shoulder into the hiding place behind the cupids. The spaces between them where they had entered were now covered with falling water, cutting off escape.

"How bad is it?" asked Horace from below.

"Real bad," she replied. "I can't see a thing through the water. I'm standing right in back of it. There's no way out."

"There must be! We came in that way."

"Not when the fountain was on, Horace. It's like being under Niagara Falls. The pressure is terrific." Niagara Falls made Judy think of her honeymoon there with Peter, and she added, "I wish Peter were here to help us. He would know what to do."

"He can help us better where he is," Horace told her when she had dropped back into the tunnel and stood on the wet floor beside him.

"But where is he?" wailed Judy. "We shouldn't

have come here without letting him know. Now we're trapped, and no one knows it except Blackberry. If he were a dog he might go for help, but cats are too independent. Of course, if Peter sees him—but will he come back today?"

"He might," Horace replied cheerfully. "Dad knows where we are. You promised to call, and if I know Dad he'll suspect something's wrong when you don't keep your promise. If he tells Peter and if they find Blackberry—"

"More *ifs*!" Judy interrupted. "Don't look so cheerful about it just because it's news. If we drowned in here that would be news, too, but we wouldn't be around to read the paper. We'll just have to find out how to shut off the water. That man must be able to control the fountain from in there. There's nothing out here that we can turn."

"There may be," Horace said. "We haven't examined the pipes."

"There isn't time!" Judy was panicky now. "You'll have to remove that drain cover before the tunnel is flooded. You should have left it open—"

"I know. I made a mistake," Horace admitted. "Now it's stuck, and I can't budge it. There's nothing to hold on to. Help me, Judy! We've *got* to get it off!"

CHAPTER XIV

A Forced Entrance

HORACE was right. There was no ring, no notch, nothing on the drain cover except a few crisscross ridges and the name of the manufacturer in an oblong box. It was what Judy used to call a skunk box when she was a little girl in Roulsville before the flood. If you stepped on one of them you were a skunk. But now the skunk box was no longer funny. Someone, evidently, had stepped on the drain cover.

"Did you, Horace?" Judy asked.

"Did I what?"

"Step on that skunk box?"

He knew what she meant. "I guess I did," he admitted. "I didn't want anyone else to trip over it the way you did. I guess I stepped on it too hard. It would take a crowbar to pry it up."

He tried working around the edge of it with his jackknife. The drain cover was slippery now that it was wet. Judy helped, prying and pushing as the water splashed down from the fountain above, getting deeper and deeper all the time. It was up to her ankles before Horace remembered having seen some lumber stacked up against the wall somewhere above the tunnel.

"If we could work a plank under the edge of that drain cover to give us leverage—" he began, but Judy had another idea.

"Why not the door? If we rammed the door to that locked room with a beam we could get in there and turn off the water before it gets any deeper. Then we could try opening the drain."

"Good idea!" agreed Horace.

First they called to the prisoner. "The drain is covered! The tunnel will be flooded if you don't turn off the fountain."

There was no answer.

Suddenly they both realized that they didn't know for sure that the man beyond the locked door had turned on the fountain. It had been a guess and they could have guessed wrong. Why didn't the man answer? Already the water was seeping in under the door. Judy banged on it, calling and shouting.

"Are you Dick Hartwell? Please, whoever you are, answer! We want to get out of here and bring help.

Do you know how to turn off the fountain?"

There was a little pause. Then came the answer.

"Outside . . . the tower!"

"Oh, no!" exclaimed Judy. "Then we are trapped unless— Is there some way to get outside from in there?" she called.

"No . . . no way." The man was evidently growing weaker. "If you really . . . want to . . . help me," he began and then broke off with a moan.

"We do want to help. Oh, Horace! We have to," cried Judy. "All three of us will be drowned if we don't get out of here!"

Horace's reply was reassuring. "Not if we succeed in opening that drain."

Another moan from behind the door spurred them to action. Horace brought a beam to push against one side of the drain cover while Judy pried up the other edge with a plank. At last it yielded to their tugging, and the water rushed and gurgled down the open drain.

The sound cheered Judy less than she had thought it would. "We're no longer in immediate danger of being drowned," she told Horace, "but you can still hear that running water in the pipes overhead. What are we supposed to do? Just wait here until they turn it off?"

"I don't like waiting any better than you do," her brother replied, "but I don't know what else we

can do. It gives me the chills just to listen to that
water. I don't trust those rusty pipes."

"You mean they might leak?"

"Some of them are already leaking," declared
Horace. "But as long as the drain is in good working
order I guess we don't have to worry too much.
The next thing to do is get dry. My feet are wet,
and I'm cold all over."

"You are shivering. Come on back to that furnace,"
Judy suggested, "before you catch your death of
cold."

She knew, from experience, that Horace caught
cold more easily than she did. But her feet were wet,
too. For a little while they stood close to the heat
of the furnace, drying themselves and wondering how
long it would be before anyone turned off the fountain.

"Maybe they leave it on all day and turn it off
at night," Horace commented.

"No, they turn it on and off whenever they feel
like it," Judy said. "When we were here yesterday
it was off in the daytime and then went on just
when it began to get dark. There's no rhyme or
reason to it unless—"

"Unless what?" asked Horace.

Judy had been afraid to say what she was thinking.

"Unless someone really *is* trying to drown us. If
the fountain is controlled from the tower, that dark

man who warned me to keep away from here might be the one who turned it on. If he saw us he knows we suspect something."

"It's news, too," lamented Horace, "but now it's too late for today's paper. It'll be in tomorrow, though. You'll see!"

"By tomorrow we'll know a lot more than we do today," Judy encouraged him. "We'll know who that prisoner is, and why he's down here. Horace, do you think he really is Dick Hartwell? Do you suppose he still wants us to go away?"

"Ask him," Horace suggested. "He should be willing to tell us who he is."

Again Judy rapped on the locked door only to hear nothing but the echo of her tapping and that unearthly rushing sound overhead.

"There is a leak," Horace told her, squinting upwards. "I knew there must be. The water would be up to our necks by now if we hadn't succeeded in opening that drain."

"Cheerful thought!" commented Judy.

She rapped on the door again—gently at first and then a little louder.

"Please answer us," she and Horace both begged.

A long, gasping moan finally came from behind the locked door.

"Are you hurt?" asked Judy. "Are you Dick Hartwell, Roger Banning's friend?"

"He's—no friend. He did it," was the confused reply.

"Now we're getting somewhere," Horace whispered. "He is willing to talk."

Judy was not so sure. "Did what?" she asked. "Did Roger Banning hurt you?"

"The time . . . what time is it?"

"He must be delirious," Horace whispered. "He doesn't understand what you said."

"What time is it?" the voice from behind the door was asking again.

Horace told him the exact time, adding that his watch was accurate. "I checked it with my car radio this morning."

"What day?"

"It's Tuesday, the third of December."

This simple statement was greeted with a moan of despair. "Eleven o'clock . . . Tuesday . . . the very day . . . the very hour!"

"Is something timed?" asked Judy, thinking that the fountain might be turned off and on by some sort of a timing device.

This sudden hope was soon dashed. The noise overhead continued the same as before except that now there was added to it a steady dripping sound from the leaky pipes. First it was in one place and then in another. Judy tried not to listen to it, but she couldn't help the feeling of panic that was mounting inside her. Horace was outwardly calm.

"What difference does it make what time it is?" Horace called.

"Too late . . ." was the only reply.

"Too late for what?" asked Judy. "Surely we can still do something."

"Report," came the voice, fainter now. "Parole officer . . . eleven today. Now they'll send me . . . back . . ."

At last Judy understood.

"You *are* Dick Hartwell, aren't you?" she asked. "You wanted to report to your parole officer, but someone shut you down here so you couldn't. Is that it?"

The answer was barely more than a sigh.

"Who did it?" asked Horace. "Was it the work of a gang of jewel thieves? I suppose they were afraid that you would report their activities, too?"

"No," the prisoner said. "They wanted . . ."

"Yes?" Horace prompted him.

Judy heard a gasp as if the man had tried to say something but hadn't breath enough left to make himself heard. He moaned, but that was all.

"It's no use, Horace," she told her brother. "He's too weak to talk."

"What do you say, sis?" he asked. "Shall I bring

that beam? The least we can do is smash our way in there and make the poor guy comfortable."

"You could try it," agreed Judy. "But you'll need a bigger beam than the one we used to open the drain."

"This will do."

The beam Horace found was so big he could hardly lift it. But together he and Judy managed to bring it. Holding the big beam between them, they both shouted, "Keep back, Dick Hartwell! We're coming through the door!"

CHAPTER XV

A Broken Water Pipe

Judy hesitated only a minute. Somehow, she felt she and Horace ought to have Dick's permission before they did anything as drastic as breaking down the door to his prison.

"Is it all right?" she called, but there was no answer.

They waited a moment more. The beam was ready, but was the prisoner ready to meet their onslaught? When there was no sound other than the rushing of water overhead and the constant *drip, drip* from the leaky pipes, they shouted a second warning.

"Keep away from the door!"

With this they rushed ahead, but on the first try they succeeded only in cracking a lower door panel.

A moan from inside told them the prisoner had been disturbed by the commotion. But still he said nothing in answer to their calls.

A second assault brought forth more moans. Judy became worried. "Let's not try that again, Horace," she pleaded. "If he's fallen against the door we could really hurt him. There must be a better way."

"If there is," her brother said, "I'm sure I can't think of it. We won't hurt him if he keeps back—"

"But can he? I'm afraid he may have fainted. The floor is all wet from those dripping pipes. If he's fallen face down in the water—"

"We have to get him out," Horace finished. "We agree on that."

"But not by hurting him." Judy's suspicions of the prisoner were forgotten. She was all sympathy now. She called gently, "We're sorry, Dick! We didn't mean to frighten you. We were just trying to get in and help—"

"Help!"

The cry sounded so faint and far away that it puzzled Judy.

"Was that only an echo?" she asked.

Horace did not answer. He was examining the crack in the lower panel. Presently he stood up, flashlight in hand.

"You may be right, sis," he said. "There may be a better way. Watch this."

Horace placed the flat of his hand against the cracked door panel and pushed with all his might. Judy heard a crack as a piece of the panel gave way and left a narrow opening through which her brother beamed his flashlight.

"Horrors!" he exclaimed. "I didn't think it was that bad. I hope we're not too late."

"Is he Dick Hartwell?"

"Take a look for yourself," he suggested, moving away from the opening. "He's in pretty bad shape, whoever he is. Dick's young, but this man looks old. Or is he? It's hard to tell under all that brush."

Judy couldn't be sure of the man's identity either. She peered through the opening in the door panel while Horace held the flashlight. There was no window in the cell-like room. There was no light at all, not even a candle. A small table, one chair and a cot in the corner were its only furnishings. Across the uncovered springs of the cot the man was sprawled, his bearded face turned toward the wall. His clothing was in tatters. He lay there motionless.

"Maybe he was telling the truth. Maybe he is dying," Judy whispered.

"Get hold of the beam and we'll smash the other door panel," Horace said urgently. "We can't hurt him if he stays over there in the corner, and maybe we can still help him. Ready?"

"I'm ready, Horace!"

He lay there motionless

"Let her go!"

This time they rammed the beam against the door with such force that both panels shattered and the beam went up like one end of a seesaw. It banged one of the pipes, and water began to pour out of it in a steady stream. Horace stared at it, his face turning pale.

"Now what have we done?" gasped Judy. "We tried to help, but just look what we've done! The tunnel will surely be flooded now!"

"The drain—will take care of it." Horace spoke jerkily and without conviction. Judy could tell that he feared the worst.

The water from the broken pipe did seem to be running toward the drain. It was icy cold. Judy wet her handkerchief in it and hurried over to the cot where the prisoner lay. She placed the handkerchief on his forehead, wiping away the beads of cold perspiration that stood there.

"He is Dick Hartwell," she told Horace.

Her brother was about to follow her through the opening they had broken in the door, but she called to him, "Warm your coat to wrap around him. Take it over to the furnace and get it good and warm. He's in shock, I think. Poor Dick! What have they done to you?"

She took his hand and found it cold. He seemed to have collapsed, perhaps from fear when the water pipe burst. The thing to do was to revive him quickly. Judy began to rub his hands, trying to start the circulation. His breath came in shallow gasps. She sould scarcely feel his pulse.

"Hurry, Horace!" she called.

But Horace was already there with the warm coat. Judy threw her own coat on top of it.

"Dick! Dick!" she called. "Wake up! You have to wake up and help us. The water is pouring in here. We have to get you out!"

The man let out a long, gasping breath and opened his eyes. Judy's face must have looked like the face of an angel as the beam from Horace's flashlight fell upon it. "Where am I?" Dick asked. "Is this heaven?"

"It is not!" Horace had to laugh in spite of their predicament. "My sister says it's too far down. Is there a way out—besides that hole under the cupids, I mean? How did you get in?"

"They . . . pushed me."

"Into the fountain, you mean? We heard you moaning and thought it must be haunted. How long have you been here?" asked Judy.

"Days." Evidently Dick didn't remember how many, but Judy could imagine how long it must have seemed. He had been without food or any other comfort. This much he told them in a hoarse, whispery voice. It was hard to make out what he said.

"Who locked you in?" questioned Horace.

"Roger. You know him. He's . . . no friend . . . made me . . . lose job. Told them . . . my record. That . . . fixed me . . . gave me . . . no peace . . . anywhere. Now . . . too late!"

Talking seemed to be too much of an effort, and he broke off here, looking beseechingly at Judy.

"It's all right, Dick. We understand. You don't have to tell us any more."

"But I want to," he protested in a louder tone. "They made me . . . sign papers. When I . . . refused . . . they beat me up . . . Bad shape. Can't walk."

"We'll get you out of here somehow," Horace promised. "Who did it? Roger and Cubby?"

Dick nodded. After taking another deep breath, he added, "and Falco. He's . . . boss. He made me . . . copy signatures . . . important men."

"Can you remember any of the names you copied?"

Dick did remember a few of them. He whispered them in such a low tone that Horace had to lean close to him in order to hear. Judy heard only the water.

"It's rising!" she exclaimed. "The drain isn't carrying it away as fast as it comes in. I didn't think it would. I—"

She stopped. Horace wasn't listening. He was busy taking notes, getting Dick's story down in black and white. He had his flashlight propped up on the table. But Judy, flashing hers in the direction of the broken water pipe, saw the flood he seemed to be ignoring.

"What's the matter with you?" she cried. "Didn't you hear me? How can you sit there with your little black notebook when water is pouring in all around us? No story is that important!"

"This one is," replied Horace. He calmly removed a piece of chocolate from his pocket, unwrapped it, and handed it to the man on the cot. "Eat it slowly," he urged. "It will give you strength. You say they brought food, but wouldn't give it to you. Then what happened?"

CHAPTER XVI

A Frantic Appeal

DICK HARTWELL finished the bit of chocolate before he answered. Now he wanted to talk. He spoke as if he were unaware of any present danger. All that he was telling Horace was in the past.

"They . . . beat . . . me . . . Falco . . . inhuman . . . no pity. If he wants anything . . . he gets it . . . no matter who's hurt. It's what *he* wants. The great Falco!" Dick's voice, weak at first, was stronger now, in derision of the gang leader. "He has no use . . . for weaklings. He says I'm a weak sister!"

"Once I was called weak," Horace told him. "The boys at the newspaper office nicknamed me Sister, but I made them change their minds."

"I guess we all . . . have weak moments."

"I'm having one right now," confessed Judy. "I'm scared, and I don't care who knows it. Maybe there's an exit to the other room. If we broke down that door—"

"No use," Dick said. "I saw . . . inside. Things stored there. They . . . showed me . . . papers—"

"The ones you signed?"

"Yes . . . and more. I gave in to them . . . at first . . . before I knew . . . what they were up to. When I refused . . . to sign any more names . . . they beat me. Now they will drown me. I don't care. I want to die."

"Well, I don't," declared Judy, "and I don't want you to die, either, Dick Hartwell. You're young. You have a good life ahead of you—"

"Not now," he interrupted. "Not . . . any more."

"You do if you go straight. But first we have to get you away from this man, Falco," Judy told him. "He's the dark man, isn't he? He warned me to keep away from here, but I'm not afraid of him. Peter won't let him hurt me. You remember Peter Dobbs, don't you?"

"Yes," he said, as if it didn't matter any more. "I . . . remember."

"We're married now. I guess you knew that. Peter was here last night with another man. They'll come back—"

"To take me to prison? No! I'd rather die here . . .

Forget me. Save yourselves. Get outside . . ."

"Is there a way outside? Is there?" asked Judy
eagerly.

But Dick said he knew of no other door out of
the tunnel. He knew of no openings at all except the
chimney to the furnace and the space under the
cupids. He had been pushed in between them and
down into the tunnel when the fountain was off.

"Have to turn it off," was all he could advise.

"But you say it's turned off from the tower?"

"That's right . . . get outside . . . to the tower."

"We can't," Horace protested. "Can't you see how
impossible it is? There's no way out of here except
through the water, and the force of it would knock
us unconscious."

"Then we'll all . . . drown," the imprisoned man
gasped and fell back on the cot as if he wished it
would soon be over.

"We won't drown if I can help it," declared Judy.
"We'll haunt the fountain ourselves. We'll yell until
somebody comes and shuts it off!"

"It won't work," Horace predicted. "Nobody will
hear us except those thugs, and they'll just laugh and
let us drown."

"Blackberry's out there. He may hear us."

"You're right, sis!" exclaimed Horace. "He may be
able to find another opening."

"Is Blackberry . . . a dog?" Dick asked from the

cot. "A dog . . . might dig . . . to meet you. Shovel . . . out there . . . by the furnace. Watch it, though! Roof might . . . cave in. Better . . . to drown."

"Well, if it's a choice of ways to die," Horace said grimly, "I think I'd rather die digging."

"So would I," agreed Judy, "but aren't we being a little too morbid? Peter wouldn't let us drown. Dad wouldn't—"

"But they don't *know!*"

"That's what I mean," insisted Judy. "We'll have to get help. If we call loud enough *someone* may hear us."

"She's right," agreed Dick. "Got to . . . take . . . chance. Funny, though. Your dog . . . didn't bark."

"Blackberry isn't a dog," Judy explained. "He's a cat."

"No good . . . calling him then."

Judy feared Dick was right. Already she could see the water backing up, filling the low places in the uneven cement floor. Soon it would spread to the corner where Dick's cot was. It would creep under the cot and finally over it. Judy shuddered as she thought of what would happen after that.

"There has to be a way out," she told Horace as they started toward the furnace, wading in water over their ankles. "We'll be back," she called reassuringly to Dick Hartwell.

He seemed not to care whether they came back or not. "Forget . . . about me," he replied. "Save yourselves . . . if you can."

Judy and Horace looked at each other in the dimming light from her flash.

"We couldn't do that, could we, sis?"

"No," she replied. "It's Dad's business to save lives, and so I guess it's our business to get Dick to him. We'll be back."

The water swirling about them became warmer as they neared the furnace. They heard it sizzle against the hot iron. Before long there would be neither light nor heat in the tunnel. The water would rise to the level of the open grate and put out the fire. The batteries in their flashlights would wear out. Horace had left his with Dick Hartwell. Now Judy used hers to look for the shovel.

"I see it!" she exclaimed at last. "It's there in the coal bin. I'm going to climb up on the coal and look around. There must be a coal chute."

Finally, standing on top of the piled-up coal, Judy discovered a tiny shutter that slid open and let in a little daylight. It was about the width of the shovel and only a few inches high.

"Even Blackberry couldn't squeeze through that," she told Horace.

Just the same they both called, "Here, kitty! Kitty! Kitty!" in their most coaxing tones.

Soon the cat peered in at them and yowled in what Judy called his asking voice. "Open it a little wider," he seemed to be saying.

"We can't! Oh, Blackberry! Help us!" cried Judy. "Somebody please hear us! Help! Help!"

"We'll have to keep calling from time to time." Horace spoke as if her frantic cry had been just plain common sense. "What do you see outside?" he asked.

"Nothing much except cement. Oh dear! I hoped we'd be under the garden."

Horace climbed up and looked out. He had a good sense of direction. "We must be under the outer wall of the pool," he said. "That's about where Blackberry was sitting. No doubt he jumped down in a hurry when the fountain went on. This tunnel seems to go around it and then underneath the main fountain. I'm afraid the shovel won't be much of a help, sis. We can't widen the coal chute without cracking the cement and letting in more water."

"I guess you're right," Judy admitted. "And it's probably reinforced with something so we couldn't get through anyway. But maybe we can send Blackberry—"

"That's an idea!" Horace interrupted. "I'll write a note while you collar him. It should be easy. He's trying to get in."

While Judy struggled to get hold of the cat, Horace tore a page from his notebook and scribbled a hasty message. Judy read it without comment, fastened it to Blackberry's collar, and sent him off. The note said:

SEND HELP! CALL PETER DOBBS AND DR. BOLTON. DICK HARTWELL, MY SISTER JUDY, AND I ARE TRAPPED UNDER FOUNTAIN ON BRANDT ESTATE. IN DANGER OF DROWNING. HURRY OR WE MAY NOT GET OUT OF HERE ALIVE.

HORACE BOLTON

CHAPTER XVII

A Daring Attempt

JUDY hoped Blackberry would head straight for the main road where he would be apt to find someone who might read the note attached to his collar. Time was of the utmost importance. Horace must feel, as she did, that it was rapidly running out.

"This story is burning a hole in my pocket," he said now. "I've *got* to get it to the *Herald*. Well, at least we're trying—"

"Trying what?" cried Judy. "We're just standing here on the coal pile doing nothing. I don't call that trying."

"Maybe not," Horace said, "but it is serving. 'He also serves who only stands and waits.'"

"You and your quotations! Maybe it is serving,

but I don't like it. Maybe you like the thought of someone finding a big story in your pocket after you're dead, but I like the thought of being alive a lot better—even with empty pockets. Why is your story so important, anyway?" asked Judy. "What, exactly, did Dick Hartwell tell you?"

"He told me plenty," replied Horace. "Enough to convict the whole Falco gang of extortion as well as robbery. His story should solve Lorraine's problem—"

"Bother Lorraine!" exclaimed Judy. "If it hadn't been for her and her childish idea that she could wish away her troubles in the fountain we might not have come here—"

"And Dick Hartwell might not have been found."

Judy hadn't thought of that. But what was the good of finding him if there was no way to help him? Blackberry was, as Dick had pointed out, only a cat. The note attached to his collar might be lost or disregarded, probably the latter. Even if he delivered it to the right people it might be much too late. As for Lorraine's problem, Judy announced that, whatever it was, it couldn't compare with the problem of life and death that she and Horace and Dick were facing here inside the tunnel with the water rising.

"Perhaps not," Horace admitted, "but it is pretty serious. Dick told me that one of the signatures he forged was that of Arthur Farringdon-Pett!"

"It was!" This information really surprised Judy. "That would mean trouble for him, wouldn't it? I suppose Dick was forced to copy it?"

"Yes, it was one of the first names Falco gave him," Horace explained. "He didn't think it was too serious until he learned how it was being used. It wasn't on a bond or anything of value, Dick told me. It was only on a sales contract."

"I see. And how was it being used?"

"Dick didn't say. Shall we go back and ask him?"

"We did promise to come back."

Judy knew they had to keep that promise before the water rose much higher. It continued to pour in from the broken pipes. Apparently whoever had turned it on had no intention of shutting it off. Dick had said the fountain was controlled from the tower.

"Horace," Judy suddenly remembered, "you didn't mention the tower in your note."

"I didn't think of it," he admitted.

"That's all right," Judy told him. "I didn't think of it either until just now. Whoever finds the note will figure out something. I hope Blackberry doesn't go back to the Brandt house with it. Oh, Horace! Suppose he goes back to that room where we found him and just sits there staring at those fish!"

"They should remind him of us. Seriously," Horace pointed out, "he is only a cat. We can't expect him to have human intelligence."

"We have it. We know the fountain is turned off from the tower. If we could get out there—"

"We can't, sis. There's no use thinking about it."

"I'd like to see it once more, anyway," Judy said. "I'd like to stand up there behind those cupids and look out at the back of the waterfall. I'd like to make a wish or say a prayer or something before we go back to where Dick is. Please, Horace!"

"Well, okay," he agreed. "I'll boost you up there if you think it will do any good. You might yell for help once more while you're at it. Maybe we can still make ourselves heard."

"We can try. Even if the crooks hear us, it's better than nobody."

Horace wasn't so sure of that.

"But anyway," he said, "you'll be safer up there than down here. The water is getting deeper all the time."

Judy climbed down from the coal pile and waded bravely into the water with Horace following close behind her. They were surprised to find the water almost warm.

"You see what does it," Horace pointed out as they passed the furnace.

Judy heard it sputter as if protesting against the water that was pouring into it through the eye-like grate. It came out warm, but that wouldn't last long for the fire would soon be out. Then, thought Judy with a shudder, cold and darkness would descend upon them. The water would creep up, unseen, until it covered them . . .

"Oh, Horace!" she cried, clinging to him. "I can't bear to think of what will happen. It's colder now—and so swift!"

The drain, they saw as they approached it, was still clear. Water rushed down it in a whirlpool. It was all they could do to keep their footing. But finally they were past the worst of it. Daylight came in faintly from the opening overhead.

"Lift me, Horace!" Judy said at last. She had to raise her voice above the roaring noise from the fountain which was now directly above them. "Do you think anyone can hear me if I stand up there behind the cupids and call for help?" she shouted.

Horace doubted it and told her so.

"Down here there's an echo, but up there your voice would be drowned out by the roar of the fountain. It's haunted all right. I never expect to hear anything more frightening than that roaring water above us."

"It scares me, too," Judy admitted, "but not as much as the water from that broken pipe. If you lift me up we might yell together, me from up there and you from down here. Then, if nobody hears us, there's one more thing I might try. You won't stop me, will you?"

"That depends on what you have in mind," Horace told her. "You're the only sister I have. Don't try anything impossible."

"I won't," Judy promised, "not if I'm sure I can't make it. But I'm a pretty strong swimmer. I think I can dive through that cascade and get to the rim. Now lift me up!"

"No!" Horace protested. "It's too dangerous. What if you don't make it? The fountain will knock the breath out of you and suck you under."

"I don't think so," Judy said. "Besides, I'm so cold now that being a little colder won't matter, and I'm already soaking wet. Please, Horace, I'll have to try it."

"I don't like it a bit," Horace said. "But what can I do? I'll look after Dick Hartwell and keep his head above water if it comes to that. He wouldn't make the effort to save himself."

"No," Judy answered, "I suppose he wouldn't." Suddenly she threw her arms around her brother's neck and kissed him.

"Cut it out!" he exclaimed. "This isn't a last fare-well. Go ahead, climb up on my shoulder. I'm getting used to it by now. When you see the water you may change your mind—"

"And yell for help!" Judy finished. "I think we ought to yell, anyway, don't you?"

Horace needed no urging. He waited until Judy

was standing behind the cupids with the waterfall all around her. Then, while she called, "Help! Help! Help!" from her high perch, he joined in from below. They both shouted and called until they were hoarse, but nobody answered.

"Is it because nobody hears us or because nobody cares?" Judy wondered.

Then, suddenly, she remembered what her grandmother had once told her. "There's always Someone who cares." This thought renewed the determined spirit within her.

"Go back!" she called down to her brother. "I'll yell to you as soon as I'm safe. Oh, Horace! It will be harder for you waiting down there with the water pouring in than it will be for me going through it."

"Pick yourself up fast," he shouted. "Get to the edge of the pool and then yell good and loud. I'll be listening!"

"I will! I'll make it. I'm sure I will."

Judy kicked off her wet shoes and threw them to test the force of the water. They immediately disappeared in the foam. Now she was not so sure.

"Suppose it does knock me out," she thought with a shiver. She had left her coat behind to cover Dick Hartwell. For a moment she stood there in her sweater and slacks, hesitating. Then, hurling herself forward with all her strength, she plunged into the fountain.

CHAPTER XVIII

The Haunted Tower

WHAT happened immediately after her daring plunge into the roaring water Judy never knew. She held her breath as it struck her full force and sucked her under. Blackness and a heavy weight closed over her.

A moment later she was fighting, struggling and kicking, not knowing which way was up. The water seemed to be knocking her about as if she were a rag doll. She felt no pain when her body slapped against something hard and was then washed away from it.

"The base of the fountain!" she thought.

That meant she was through the worst of it. She could see nothing, but she could feel the hard cement base the next time the force of the water threw her against it. Doubling herself up and then giving a tremendous push away from it, she was again at the mercy of the foaming spray. Fighting, fighting, she came at last to the surface of the water and gulped a breath of fresh air.

"How did I get way out here?" she wondered, opening her eyes and blinking in the unexpected sunshine. To her surprise, she was already halfway across the pool that surrounded the main fountain. She had been fighting and thrashing around in the water without realizing that she was swimming. Now it seemed too much of an effort. She still had to pass the stone lions.

"They're roaring at me," she thought unreasonably.

She tried to swim around the cold shower from the lion's mouth, but now the roaring noise grew louder, and she realized it must be inside her own head.

"I'm hurt! I can't swim another stroke!" one part of her seemed to be saying.

But another part of her mind kept urging, "You must swim! You must get help! Horace and Dick Hartwell are still down there in the tunnel with the water pouring in! You must hurry, hurry and turn off the fountain!"

The sight of the tower encouraged her. It did not seem so far away. Once she was out of the water she had only to run a short distance and turn whatever had to be turned.

"How will I know?" she wondered.

The sickening thought came to her that she knew nothing of pipes and valves and would have no idea what to turn. It made her feel weak. "It's no use," she told herself. "I won't know!"

"You must know! Hurry, hurry!" the second voice inside her persisted until finally she struck out with a few long strokes that took her quickly to the edge of the pool. Pulling herself up with a final, determined effort, she cupped her hands and shouted hoarsely, "I made it, Horace! I'm—all—right!"

But was she? It had hurt her to call. It even hurt to breathe. She had held her breath for so long that now it was easier not to let it out. A great weight seemed to be sitting on her chest. Her whole body was stiff and numb with cold. Her torn clothing seemed to be plastered to it. She shook herself like a wet puppy and tilted her head first one way and then another to get rid of the roaring in her ears. Hearing no answer to her call, she called again.

"This is Judy! I got through! Can you hear me down there? Are you all right?"

Still she could hear nothing but the roaring of the fountain with its stone lions glaring angrily at her and spitting out foam.

"I got through it!" she cried, her voice cracking with the effort. "Can you hear me?"

"Hear you!" sounded faint and far away as if it came from the fountain itself.

"The spirit!" whispered Judy. It gave her a shivery feeling of excitement. The fountain, in spite of its terrors, was still beautiful. It was hard to imagine Horace trapped under it. "That must be his voice," she told herself. "I know who the spirit is this time, but who was it the other time so long ago?"

She couldn't just sit beside the pool wondering. Pulling herself to her feet, she found it hurt her to stand. And yet she must hurry to the tower and turn off the water before it was too late.

"Is Dick all right?" she shouted, and the shout came back like an echo.

"All—right!"

Was it an echo? Judy did not know and decided not to take time to find out. Time was precious. She couldn't waste it, and yet, oh, how it hurt her when she tried to walk! It felt as if she had icicles attached to her body instead of legs. And yet she must move them. She must make herself do it.

"Hurry! Hurry!" she whispered as if the words were enough to speed her along the path to the tower. She ran stiffly with a limp that grew worse as she neared the tall stone edifice.

"It mustn't be locked!" she cried. "That would be too cruel."

She found the lock broken and the great door sagging on rusty hinges that creaked as she opened it. Inside there was nothing except a great, gloomy round room that looked as if it had been built on purpose to house witches and owls and bats. She even fancied she could hear them fluttering. It reminded her of a giant bell tower only, instead of a bell, she looked up to see a huge tank supported by steel girders.

Was the thing she had to turn up there? The tank could be reached by narrow, wooden steps that wound up and up until, near the top, there was only a ladder.

"This is the end!" thought Judy. "I can never climb it."

But would it be necessary to climb all the way up to the tank in order to turn off the fountain? A steady, whispering noise drew her attention to what looked like an electric motor with a switch above it. Not at all sure what would happen, she reached up and turned off the switch.

"Now what have I done?" she asked herself as the whole tower shuddered and sighed. A moan came from the great storage tank overhead. Not only the fountain, but the tower, too, seemed to be haunted.

The whispering and moaning continued for less

than a minute. The silence that followed let Judy breathe again. The electric motor was still.

"I did it!" she thought with sudden elation. But was shutting off the motor enough? "If this is an electric pump then it probably pumps water into that big storage tank overhead," she reasoned, "and if the tank is still full it will continue to pour water into the tunnel until it empties itself, and that may be too late!"

Judy was seized with the fear that already it was too late to save Dick Hartwell. But Horace could swim. He might keep himself from drowning until he reached the entrance under the cupids, but he could never dive through the cascade as she had done. Somehow, she must turn off the fountain.

"Is this the right valve?" she wondered.

She had discovered a number of pipes leading down from the tank. Pipes always confused her. Several of them had valves that she could turn. None of the valves were marked. A mistake might be costly, but indecision was worse. Judy began turning off all the valves she could find, one after the other.

"That ought to do it." In the excitement of turning the valves she had forgotten her cold and discomfort. Now she was eager to get out of the gloomy tower and into the sunshine. But just as she was about to leave she discovered still another pipe ending in a plunger marked: DRAIN.

"That's it!" she cried, and her voice echoed back to confirm her feeling that now she had made the tunnel safe for her brother and the poor, hurt prisoner, Dick Hartwell. "This must drain the pool," she reasoned as she lifted the plunger. "Now they'll be —safe!"

After it was done she sank against the stone wall exhausted, but still with the feeling that there was something urgent that she had to do.

"I must go back to the fountain and help Horace," she told herself, but she was too weak to make the effort. Her eyes closed, but in another moment they flew open. Someone was shaking her roughly by the shoulder and shouting, "What's the big idea, you? You've shut off all the water in the house! What're you doing here, anyway?"

"The water? The house?" Judy tried to collect her thoughts, but all she could think of was the fountain with the water still pouring into the tunnel out of the broken pipe. She was there again, shivering in the icy cold water. But it didn't matter any more. All she could say was, "I'm cold. Go away! Let me sleep!"

CHAPTER XIX

Falco

THE man shook her again. Judy stared at him, recognizing him as Falco, the gangster who had warned her to keep away from the estate he and his thieving friends seemed to have taken over. Fortunately, he did not recognize her in her torn slacks and soggy sweater. Her clinging, wet hair probably didn't look the same color as it had the day before.

"Did you say . . . I turned off the water in the house?" she questioned dazedly.

"Yes, and everywhere else! Now beat it before you do any more damage. Wait! What did you want, anyway?" he asked menacingly.

"I've been in the water, as you can see," Judy replied. "Weren't you pretty sure there was somebody down underneath the fountain when you turned it on? Or weren't you the one who turned it on?"

"Me?" He seemed surprised. "Why would I do a thing like that?"

"I'm asking you. Why would you?" Judy retorted. "You might have drowned me. Or were you *trying* to drown someone?"

"I'm surprised," he said, smiling slyly, "that you could think such a thing. If anyone gets drowned down there it will be a most unfortunate accident. Of course," he added, "we have been bothered by prowlers lately. People get curious about a place like this. It's not always healthy for them. But I guess you found out that much."

"I didn't find out nearly as much as I'd like to," declared Judy, the heat of her anger warming her a little. "Were you trying to drown somebody? We were down under it when the water was turned on. I thought we were trapped at first, but I managed to get through the cascade and turn all these valves. I didn't mean to shut off the water at the house," she hurried on to explain. "I only meant to turn off the fountain."

"You turned it off all right," he told her, "but you wasted your time. We like it on!"

With that he began turning one of the valves, but

Judy caught his hand and bent it behind him, crying hysterically as she held it in a tight grip, "No! No! You mustn't turn it on! You did it before, but I won't let you do it again. I'll hold both your hands and yell if you try it!"

"No, you won't! I'll do the yelling. Edith!" he shouted as he tried unsuccessfully to shake Judy off and turn the valve. The same determination that had carried her through the water was giving her almost savage strength.

"Get her away!" Falco shouted to a dark-haired woman who now came running through the half-open door and stopped abruptly, an amused expression coming over her face. "What's the matter with you?" he cried. "Edith! Don't just stand there. Grab her!"

"Oh-oh, so it's you again," the newcomer said, staring at Judy. "Mister," she added, sneering at Falco, "I think you're in trouble. Way in!"

"What do you mean I'm in trouble?"

The valve forgotten, Falco whirled on the dark woman and demanded an explanation. Judy had to release his hands, but she still kept close watch to make sure he did not turn on the fountain. Now she knew which valve was the right one. Whatever it cost her, she intended to make sure it was not turned. Falco was paying little attention to her now. His anger was directed elsewhere.

"This little hobo wouldn't have jumped me if I'd

had my gun," he said furiously to the woman called
Edith.

"What happened to it?" she asked. "Did the big
bad G-man take it away from you?"

Peter did it! This thought cheered Judy in spite
of her predicament. If Peter suspected the Brandt
estate was being used as a gang hideout, he'd be back.

Falco's voice rose angrily. "Think I need a gun to
take care of her? I'll stop her—"

"Unless she stops you first," the woman informed
him. "She and her brother came to the house this
morning. Said they wanted to interview someone.
I didn't see them, but I heard them talking to
Stanley. She wanted to meet someone of importance.
Well, she's met the great Falco. He's someone of
importance. Anyway, *he* thinks so."

"None of your cracks," the gang leader warned.
"Is this true?" he demanded, turning to Judy. "Were
you and your brother at the house this morning?"

"We were," she replied fearlessly, "and so were the
police."

"They had a search warrant," the woman put in.
"I told them to go ahead and search the house. Naturally, they didn't find anything. We're friends of the
Brandts, living in their house while they're on vacation. It was as simple as that."

"What about the fountain?" Falco demanded.

"They didn't go near it. They only searched the

tower. I showed them around myself when I saw them heading for it. And while I was there with them I turned on the fountain."

"You turned it on?" cried Judy, unable to control her feelings any longer. "Then *you're* to blame for what happened!"

"What did happen?" asked Falco.

"Nothing," replied the woman, who, Judy realized, must be Mrs. Cubberling. "They thanked me and drove away."

"Then why do you say I'm in trouble?"

"Because of her!" Mrs. Cubberling pointed a finger at Judy.

"I can take care of her—easy. But first I want to hear her side of the story. She hasn't told me why she came here."

"Today or yesterday?" asked Judy, trying to confuse him.

"Were you here yesterday, too?" Falco demanded. "But of course you were! I warned you not to come back. Can't you read? There's a sign down the road warning trespassers away. My men tell me a car drove right past it yesterday. There were two girls in it. Were you one of them?"

"What if I was?" asked Judy, glad that he had not noticed Lorraine when she ducked. Suddenly Judy became aware of the seriousness of her situation.

"Speak up!" the gang leader barked. "Why did you

come here? And I do mean today. I want the truth."

"You'll get it," Judy said quietly, her hand still on
the valve to keep him from turning it. "It's exactly
the way she told you. I came with my brother to get
a story. He has a weekly column in the *Farringdon
Daily Herald*. It's called 'Meet Your Neighbor,' and
we decided that you were a neighbor the public might
like to meet. We wanted an interview. That was all.
We were going to ask about your business, your
hobbies—things like that."

"Go ahead, Falco! Tell her your hobbies." Edith
Cubberling laughed mockingly. "You have a lot of
them."

"I haven't time to listen," Judy said hurriedly, not
liking the ugly tone of voice the woman was using.
"I have to go back to the fountain—"

"Oh, no, you don't!" said Mrs. Cubberling, her
stocky frame blocking the doorway.

"She has to go back!" Falco tipped back his head
and laughed. "Did you hear that, Edith? She's half
drowned and shivering with cold, but she has to go
back to the fountain!"

Judy was still guarding the valve when the woman
sprang forward with the ferocity of a tiger and
pushed her away from it.

"This will teach you not to go poking around
where you're not wanted," she snarled as she struck
Judy sharply across the cheek.

"This will teach you not to go poking
around where you're not wanted!"

The blow was so unexpected that it knocked Judy off her feet and sent her spinning into a corner where she lay helpless.

"That'll hold you for a while," the gang leader told her. "Come on, Edith! We have to take care of her brother if the water hasn't already done it."

CHAPTER XX

A Passing Shadow

"Wait!" cried Judy. Anything, she thought, to thwart their deadly plans. She knew now that her strength was not enough, but if she could only give Horace more time, keep this evil pair away from the fountain—"They mustn't know they've hurt me," she told herself. "I'll keep on talking. I'll keep on stalling them. But, please God, let help come soon!"

Already exhausted and chilled to the bone, Judy had scarcely felt the vicious blow. From sheer fatigue she was unable to pick herself up from where she had fallen, but there were other ways to stop them.

"There's something I ought to tell you," she called, hoping to, at least, delay them and give Horace a chance to escape and drag Dick Hartwell to safety while the fountain was still turned off.

"She has something to tell us. Don't you want to hear it?" Edith Cubberling asked.

"If it's something about the fountain, we already know it," Falco informed her.

"Yes, and so does she. I could have told Roger Banning she'd find out there was a fountain on the estate. He said she was asking about it yesterday."

"I suppose he was just fool enough to tell her!"

"He didn't need to tell me where it was," Judy spoke up bravely. "I remembered. I was here once before with my grandparents and heard it speak."

"The fountain—spoke?"

Now at last she had them interested.

"Yes," she replied, trying a desperate bit of strategy. "Surely you know it's haunted!"

"Haunted? What rubbish is this?" demanded Mrs. Cubberling.

"But it really is." Judy did not need to pretend the effective shiver that accompanied this statement. "We heard moans coming from it and found out that it speaks whenever anyone is trapped under it. I know, because I heard it speak in my brother's voice."

"Did you hear any other voices?" Falco wanted to know.

"I did hear moans," Judy answered guardedly. "Or didn't I tell you? Of course, you wouldn't know anything about the poor, dying man we found imprisoned under the fountain."

"You—found him?" Falco had stopped dead still to listen.

"She's talking nonsense," Mrs. Cubberling said in an offhand way. "Come on. Let's get going!"

"Wait! I want to hear this. The girl may have something to tell us, at that," Falco said.

"The man looked very miserable," Judy went on significantly. "He was wearing ragged clothes, and he had a heavy black beard."

"You—saw him?" they both gasped.

"Of course," replied Judy. "He was right there on the cot. My brother and I both saw him. It wasn't a pretty sight."

Falco and Mrs. Cubberling exchanged glances. "Did he talk at all?" Falco asked.

"He moaned. I told you that. We heard him moaning and thought the fountain was haunted. That's how we happened to explore it."

"You explored it all right. Now we'll explore it ourselves and find out how you got in there!"

"But I can tell you. We got in through the door!"

They both stared at Judy as if she were a spirit. Falco was the first to recover himself. He turned on his companion. "Did you leave that door unlocked?"

"No," Mrs. Cubberling snapped. "You must have."

"Maybe he unlocked it himself." Falco laughed unpleasantly and added, "I told you we'd been bothered by prowlers. Is it our fault what happens to them?"

"I think what happened to this man was your fault," replied Judy. She was about to mention the beating and then thought better of it. After all, she was just stalling until help came. It would be better to mention something they didn't already know. There was that broken water pipe, for instance. "Of course," she added, "it wasn't entirely your fault. Part of it was accidental. One of the pipes broke and poured water into the room—"

"Which room?" they both interrupted.

"The room where we found the prisoner," Judy answered. "We broke the pipe by accident when we rammed in the door."

"You rammed it in? You—you—" Falco was stuttering in his anger. "What about the other door?"

"Oh!" said Judy as if she had just remembered it. "That's right. There was another door."

"Did you go in that room, too?" He looked ready to kill her if she had. Judy couldn't help wondering what secret that other door was hiding.

"We didn't bother with it," she replied truthfully. "There wasn't time. The water was pouring in. I managed to escape, but my poor brother is still down there with that dead man."

Falco gasped. "Dead man, did you say?"

It flashed across Judy's mind that it might be safer for Falco to think Dick Hartwell was dead. He mustn't know Dick had talked. She thought of his story, now in Horace's pocket, and her brother's words, "I can keep his head above water if it comes to that."

"He's dead now," she replied in a hoarse whisper. Her voice was leaving her. She couldn't keep talking much longer. What she had told them could easily be the truth. She coughed painfully and added, "My brother probably is dead by now, too, but I guess that doesn't matter to you. The contents of that room down there is all that matters, isn't it?"

"What do you know about the contents of that room?" snarled Mrs. Cubberling. She turned to Falco and said almost triumphantly, "See? I told you you're in trouble!"

"Answer her!" Falco commanded Judy.

Judy tried to answer, but only a croak came out. Finally she managed to tell them she knew nothing. It was true. She had been making wild guesses. She had guessed, by the way they were acting, that the contents of the locked room meant more to them than human lives. Now there was nothing she could say to stop them from going back there to protect their treasure.

"Please, Horace, if you escape, go the other way!" Judy whispered.

"What's she saying, Edith? I can't hear her."

"No wonder," the woman answered. "She's so hoarse now she can't speak above a whisper."

Falco gave an evil chuckle. Judy saw Mrs. Cubberling looking at him as if she might be seeing him for the first time.

"I don't believe they'd ram in one door without having a try at the other," he continued, "but she could be telling the truth."

"Some people do. I'd nearly forgotten." The woman's voice sounded almost wistful. It changed abruptly as she added, "I suppose you're going to ask me to get the truth out of her?"

"Not now! Keep it quiet!" he warned. "I think I hear someone outside. It could be the police."

Judy hoped it was.

"If it is the police, it's your own fault!" Mrs. Cubberling snarled at Falco. "I told you one of these days they'd catch up with you. Today may very well be the day. You've bungled this job from start to finish!"

"But you're in it, too—"

"I'd have the satisfaction," she interrupted, "of seeing you get yours, and I'd be as free in prison as I am in this gang working for you. I'm through, as of this minute!"

"What do you mean you're through?"

"I mean I'm through—fed up—finished! I've done all the dangerous work for you and my husband long enough. Maybe I'd like someone who'd take care of *me* for a change. Maybe *I'd* like to wear some of those precious rubies and diamonds—"

"Quiet!" commanded Falco. "Someone's coming!"

A figure passed the door on a run, but Judy saw only his shadow. Mrs. Cubberling rushed over to one of the peepholes in the tower.

"Know him?" asked Falco.

"No, but I'll bet this girl does. He's in a big hurry, and he's on his way to the fountain. We'd better follow him."

"It won't do you any good to yell," the gang leader warned Judy as they started off. "Someone's sure to get hurt if you do."

CHAPTER XXI

Tragic News

JUDY paid little attention to the ugly threat. She had no idea who the man was. The shadow that had passed the tower door had been misshapen and fleeting, but it gave her hope.

"It could be a policeman—or Peter."

She thought of Cubby and immediately recoiled from the thought. But it *had* looked like the shadow of a stout man. Peter was not stout. Neither was Horace and, anyway, Horace could hardly be running past the tower toward the fountain. If he were running at all he would be running away from it to get help.

"It must be someone coming to help him," Judy decided.

She would not let herself believe it was Cubby or any other member of Falco's gang. They had been cruel to Dick Hartwell. Horace could expect no mercy from them. In her thoughts Judy could hear what they had said to each other all over again. Edith Cubberling's threat to quit the gang meant nothing unless she could take the treasure with her. "Maybe I'd like to wear some of those precious rubies and diamonds," she had said.

Could Lorraine's ruby be in the collection? In spite of her cold and discomfort, Judy found herself still trying to solve her friend's problem. It kept her from thinking about her own. But if the ruby had been stolen, why was Lorraine afraid to say so? Was it because of some ugly threat to her life or the life of someone she loved? Arthur, for instance. But that didn't make sense, either. She'd called Arthur a cheat. His name had been forged. Judy mustn't forget that. It might be a clue to the whole mystery.

"I'll tell Peter. He'll figure it out. Oh, why doesn't he come? I need help. I can't move without feeling chilly all over. If only someone would bring me my coat!"

Judy tried to think where she had left it, and suddenly it all came back to her. The coat she needed so much was back there under the fountain, covering Dick Hartwell. All at once she thought of the diamond she had found. She had tied it in the corner of

her handkerchief and put it in her coat pocket. Was
it still there? Judy didn't care any more. She almost
wished she had never found it in the first place.

"A frozen tear!" she thought, "and now I'm nearly
frozen! Where is Blackberry?" The warmth of the
cat's soft fur would be some comfort even if he
hadn't delivered their message. But perhaps he had!
The tower hadn't been mentioned. Whoever came in
answer to Horace's SOS would hurry right to the
fountain.

"It will be safe now. Falco didn't turn it back on!
I did one thing," Judy told herself. "I kept them from
turning that valve. They threatened me on purpose
to make me afraid of them, but they're the ones who
have the most to fear. I'll be all right in a minute, and
then I'll follow them and see who that man was."

The minute passed. Another followed it and then
another. More shadows passed by the door, but when
Judy opened her mouth to call to them nothing came
out, not even a hoarse croak.

"I'll have to get outside where Peter can see me,"
she decided. She was so used to having him come
when she needed him that she couldn't believe her
helplessness now. There was no pain in her bruised
foot, but she simply could not stand on it no matter
how bravely she tried. Suddenly she was seized with
a violent chill. It was all she could do to drag herself
from the gloomy tower out into the sunshine.

The day was sunny but cold. It was the penetrating cold of early December. Judy's wet clothing had started to freeze while she was still in the tower. Now it felt as if she were encased in ice like a mummy.

"This can't be happening to me," she thought.

Never, in her whole life, had she felt so alone and helpless. She felt it was her own fault, too, for not calling Peter and telling him where she was going. But wouldn't Honey tell him? She knew, and so did her father. Didn't anyone care?

Tears filled Judy's eyes and ran down her cheeks. But they fell into no enchanted fountain. "It wasn't enchanted. It was haunted. I wish I'd never seen it. I wish—"

As if in answer to her wish she heard the sound of a twig breaking. Someone was coming along the path from the fountain. Judy's heart began hammering in anticipation. Even Falco would be better than nobody. But would he? To her dismay, it was the gang leader's voice she heard.

"We can't get near it," he was snarling. "The police have it roped off. They'll search every inch of it, and we're helpless, thanks to you!"

"Why me?" asked Mrs. Cubberling. "Why blame everything on me? It's that redheaded girl. She wasn't as weak as we thought she was. She's gone!"

Evidently they hadn't seen Judy. Maybe it was just as well, but somebody had to see her! She knew now that her strength was not enough, that she would have to attract the attention of the police who had come to rescue Horace and Dick Hartwell. Had they been in time?

"They can't let me just lie here and die," thought Judy. She had never thought very much about dying. She had always felt so vibrantly alive. But now, suddenly, it seemed possible. And yet help must be very near. Falco had mentioned the police. He and Edith Cubberling were now hiding inside the tower. If they climbed the stairs and crawled into the big tank it would make an even better hiding place, now that it was empty. But now the voices suddenly sounded nearer.

"Look!" Falco exclaimed. "She didn't get away. I told you she couldn't. There she is lying on the ground. Just wait till I get my hands on her!"

He started for Judy, but Mrs. Cubberling screamed at him. "You fool! Don't you touch her! Do want to get us all sent up for life? The place is surrounded! You have enough crimes to answer for already. If you have any sense you'll give yourself up and send that man we followed back here. He says he's a doctor."

"Yeah? He also says someone found a cat with a note on its collar and telephoned him. I suppose you fell for that, too."

"Why not?" she replied. "If it's the same black

cat I caught prowling around here last night, it came with that G-man who traced the phone call. He's this girl's husband. Didn't you hear him asking about her?"

"Peter! He's come!" Judy whispered.

"What's that?" Falco questioned, leaning closer. "What do you know about that cat?"

"Where—is he?" croaked Judy.

"I don't know, but I'd kill him if I could find him. It's bad enough to be trapped by a girl, but a *cat!*" He spat out the word and made a violent gesture.

"And a black cat at that. I've always heard they were bad luck," put in Mrs. Cubberling, "especially this one. He belongs to Judy Bolton, of course. Yes, I've guessed her name. Roger Banning told us about her, remember? Her family moved into the house where old Vine Thompson used to operate. Roger said this girl and her brother helped Chief Kelly round up most of the gang, and Roger said they'd get you, too. It was when you held the gun on him and made him bring us his friend with the prison record. I'd like to see you talk yourself out of this mess when that G-man finds this girl."

"Let him!" growled Falco. "We didn't hurt her. She hurt herself diving into the fountain. It was turned on full force. I don't see how she ever got through it. That water has power. For my money it was all the protection we needed."

"If Dick Hartwell is dead—" Edith Cubberling began.

"He's dead all right. Real dead," Falco interrupted, "but I don't have to answer for that. *You* turned on the fountain, Edith. I'm not forgetting that."

"Don't think you're going to blame everything on me!" she screamed. "And you're not going to get me in any deeper! I'm going back there and get that doctor. But not until you clear out. I don't trust you. 'If anyone goes near that fountain, turn it on!' you said, and so I turned it. But is that man back there real dead, as you say, or isn't he? It makes a big difference. They were still working over him when we left."

"That's routine," declared Falco. "The doctor was just pulling two of them out of the pool when we caught up with him. 'Neither one of them will do much talking,' he said. Both drowned, I guess."

"Do you think the other one was her brother?"

"Horace—drowned? Oh, no!" gasped Judy. "It can't be true!"

"What's she saying?" asked Falco. "Maybe we've still got a chance if we listen."

"Don't be a fool! It was listening to all her made-up talk about a haunted fountain that spoiled our chances," declared Edith Cubberling. "I'm going for her father. You hide in the empty tank. They'll never find you there!"

"What if she tells them where I am?"

"She won't. She's unconscious. She won't bother you."

Moments elapsed in which Judy was dimly aware of retreating footsteps. The last thing she heard was Edith Cubberling's triumphant chuckle. "Don't worry, my dear," she seemed to be saying, "Falco won't bother you either."

CHAPTER XXII

Afterwards

MANY hours later Judy opened her eyes and looked up to see Peter standing beside her bed. His blue eyes were regarding her anxiously. His face came into focus.

"Peter!" she gasped.

"I'm here, Angel. I've been waiting for you to wake up. How are you feeling?"

"Hot," she said. "That's funny! I was so cold before. Is it a fever?" She looked around the room and saw that she must be in a hospital. An oxygen tank was also standing beside her bed, but the funny little cage was no longer over her nose. "I guess I was pretty sick," she concluded.

"You were pretty brave," Peter said, his voice husky.

A nurse she knew came in quietly. Judy moved her foot experimentally and discovered that it was in a cast.

"Oh!" she said. "No wonder I couldn't walk. I guess I broke it against the fountain." Then, all at once, her nightmare experience rushed back to her and she added sorrowfully, "It was no use. I limped back to the tower as fast as I could and turned off all the valves I could find—but it was all for nothing. I still can't believe it, Peter. Horace—drowned—"

"Who said so?" Peter interrupted quickly. "Why, Horace is in the room right next to this one. He's in better shape than you are. They even let him have a typewriter. Hear it?"

Judy listened a moment. She had never heard a sweeter sound.

"That brother of mine!" she said with tears in her eyes. "I guess he's polishing up that story he had in his pocket."

"Wrong again, Angel!" Peter was smiling at her now and holding her hand. "That story is already spread all over the front page of the paper. You'll read it as soon as your father thinks you're strong enough. You have a lot of catching up to do."

"I know. I still feel weak when I think of it. Falco said something about two dead men, and I guess I fainted or something. Peter, he's hiding in the water tower—"

"Not any more," Peter broke in gently. "He was fished out of the tank, half drowned himself. Edith Cubberling told us where he was, but not until after she'd turned on the pump and the tank started to fill up. He had a taste of his own medicine. She was following his orders, she says, when she turned on the fountain. If it hadn't been for you and that blessed cat of yours, Angel—"

"Please," Judy stopped him, laughing a little and feeling more like herself. "Angels don't keep black cats, or go exploring under fountains."

"Your kind of angel," Peter told her, "goes wherever she's needed. I ought to scold you for rushing headlong into danger. I've warned you again and again that the FBI deals with dangerous criminals and that I don't want you involved—"

"Please, Peter, believe me. I didn't know it was dangerous. I didn't know you were investigating anything at the Brandt estate until I found Blackberry and heard Stanley say two government men had been there. Then it made sense. I thought you had brought him."

"And I thought you had."

Judy sighed and gave up. "I guess Blackberry himself is the only one who really knows why he went there. You did let him out of the attic, didn't you? I hope he'll forgive me for shutting him up there. I thought you'd find him."

"I did." Peter didn't say when. "I went up there to investigate a noise I heard, and there was poor Blackberry all tangled up in your sewing things. I unwound him and let him out the front door, and away he went! The next thing I knew he was looking at me from the front page of the paper."

"They photographed him? Oh, Peter! How wonderful. Whose idea was it?"

"Well, you might say it was your brother's. He thought it would please you. He said black cats deserved a little favorable publicity. He even quoted what you once said about Blackberry being unlucky for criminals. It was certainly true of Falco. The whole gang is being arraigned in court tomorrow morning. They're all willing to talk, even the Cubberlings. That woman has been talking a blue streak ever since we picked her up."

"You know why, don't you?"

"Well, no," Peter replied in a puzzled voice. "I can't say that I do."

"She thought she had murdered two persons by turning on the fountain," Judy explained. "She did it on his orders. She told Falco she'd be as free in prison as she was working for him."

"This has taught her a lesson then." Peter's grip on her hand tightened as he added, "You taught me one, too. I know now you'll never be a meek little housewife who will stay home and dust the furniture while

I go out solving the world's problems. You'll be right there solving them with me."

"It wasn't the world's problems I set out to solve," Judy objected. "It was only Lorraine's. She seemed so troubled. She doesn't trust Arthur. It's a terrible thing for a girl who's still practically a bride to be haunted with fear and suspicion the way she is."

"I know," Peter replied. "Arthur had told me. We had quite a talk one night. When you went to the movies with Honey, I can tell you now, I spent that evening with Arthur, too. We traced a telephone call from Lorraine and confirmed his suspicions. She went back there to the Brandt estate and gave Falco more of her jewelry."

"So that was what happened to her ruby? Why did she do it, Peter?"

"That," he replied, "is something I had been hoping Lorraine would tell you herself."

"She didn't. Lois said she had a problem, but she wouldn't tell me a thing about it. I didn't notice that her ruby was gone until I found that diamond. Was it still in my coat pocket?" Judy asked.

"It was." Peter looked at her a long moment and then added, "It was still tied in the corner of your handkerchief. I found it before I found you. But now you've talked enough. I'd better leave and let you get some rest."

"I can listen, can't I? Tell me more, Peter. Tell me

what's in the paper. Can't I see Blackberry's picture?"

Peter hesitated. Judy saw an anxious expression on his face. He went out, and after quite a few minutes he returned with her father. He also had a copy of the *Farringdon Daily Herald*.

"Just one peek!" Dr. Bolton said after he had checked Judy's breathing and given her an injection. "I didn't expect you to recover quite this fast," he admitted. "You really had us worried for a while, Judy girl."

"I know, Dad." Judy wanted to say more, but the words wouldn't come. Peter spread the paper before her. She looked at the picture of her precious pet for a long time before she asked, "What's that white thing on his paw?"

"It's a cast," Peter told her. "He wanted to imitate his mistress, so your father put a cast on him, too. Seriously, a car hit him. Don't worry! Only his paw was hurt."

"Poor Blackberry! I wonder if he walked out into the road on purpose so someone would see him," mused Judy. "We didn't think he'd be much help to us at first, Dad. But he did carry our message. Horace wrote it, and I tucked it under his collar. We were lucky he had the collar on. I was going to wait until Christmas to give it to him and have his name engraved on it, but it looked so cute. Dogs have collars, and I think collars make cats look important, too."

"Blackberry doesn't need to look important. He *is* important," Dr. Bolton said.

"I know," his mistress agreed. "He could tell we were in danger. Cats hate water anyway, and when he saw us trapped by it he was right there waiting until we needed him. It is a shame, though. We tried so hard to save Dick Hartwell. He said he wanted to die—"

"Your father disappointed him then," Peter broke in, smiling. "He's alive but still on the critical list. It looks now as if he might pull through."

Judy could hardly believe she had been in time to save Dick, too. "I don't understand this at all," she said a little later. "Why would Falco think they were drowned if they were really alive? Dad must have told him they were dead. Why?"

"Perhaps he'd better tell you." Peter kissed Judy lightly on the forehead. "Did I tell you how brave you were, chatterbox? Did I tell you how much I love you?"

"You showed me," Judy said. "You came and rescued me, didn't you? I thought it was a dream, but after I fainted I seemed to feel myself in your arms. Peter, is Dad—"

"He is," Dr. Bolton interrupted before Judy could finish asking the question.

"Then everything is all right," Judy said, and closed her eyes.

CHAPTER XXIII

Lorraine's Confession

EVERYTHING was not all right, as Judy soon discovered. When she awoke Peter was not there, and neither was her father. She had a younger nurse—a student whom she did not know. "Are you feeling well enough to have visitors today?" the nurse was asking. "Mr. and Mrs. Farringdon-Pett are here to see you."

"Arthur! Lorraine!" exclaimed Judy as they came in. "I'm happy—so happy you came together."

She did not ask if their differences were all mended. Lorraine said simply, "We've been talking with Horace."

"How is he?" asked Judy. "The sound of his type-writer has been like music—"

"Not to me," Lorraine interrupted.

Arthur gave her one of his frosty looks and answered Judy's question. "He looks about the same as usual. He was treated for shock and submersion and sent home."

Judy laughed. "I am in a fog. I don't even know what day it is."

"Time passes quickly in a hospital. It seems ages since we had luncheon together. Did you know Arthur had asked Peter to arrange it?" Lorraine asked. "Arthur didn't trust me, either, I guess. He's always arranging things for me. But we don't want to burden you with our troubles. We brought you some flowers."

"Oh, thank you!" exclaimed Judy. She took the roses Arthur gave her and breathed in their fragrance. "I can breathe now," she told him, "without that awful pain in my chest. Dad says I'll be as good as new before long, and so will Horace. But how are you, Lorraine? You were so frightened the last time I saw you."

"I'm still frightened. Oh, Judy! Judy!" cried Lorraine. "How can I ever explain things to Arthur?"

"What is there to explain?" he asked coldly. "Peter has given me all the facts."

"I don't mean facts!" Lorraine cried. "You see, Judy, he doesn't understand. He doesn't want to listen when I try to tell him. He says he's heard enough about that terrible gangster. He could have killed you, Judy—"

"He didn't, Lorraine. I'm very much alive."

"He killed something else then. He killed Arthur's love for me. That beautiful ring was a symbol of his love, and I gave it to that awful man. I thought I had to keep him quiet. I don't expect either of you to believe it, but when Falco telephoned me and made all those threats, I thought he'd expose Arthur and the whole family would be disgraced if I didn't give him the ruby. Then he said it wasn't enough, and I went back and gave him more of my jewelry. He called himself Falco and said he was fighting crime."

"Who was I?" asked Arthur. "The criminal?"

"Well, no—not exactly, but he did make me think you were cheating people, misrepresenting everything, building all those new houses in Roulsville and even the Farringdon post office, out of defective materials."

"You believed all that—of me, Lorraine?"

She admitted it with a nod. Tears were streaming down her face. Judy tried to comfort her. But she said the wrong thing. She mentioned the ring, only to learn that the police had been unable to recover any of the jewelry Lorraine had foolishly given to Falco.

"That ruby has caused a lot of grief," Arthur said

bitterly. He seemed stunned by Lorraine's confession. They kept looking at each other as if they were strangers instead of the devoted couple Judy had believed them to be. Finally Arthur said, "We'd better go now. We shouldn't have upset you with our problems, Judy. May I apologize for both of us?"

Lorraine was still crying when they left. The nurse hurried in with Dr. Bolton. She said something to him about the visitors being bad for patients and he agreed. Judy did feel weak. She was glad when visiting hours were over and she could rest.

Lorraine was alone the next time she came to visit Judy. In the meantime Judy's mother, Peter's grandparents, his sister Honey, and many of Judy's friends and neighbors had been in to see her. Horace had visited her while he was still in the hospital, but now he was out on the trail of more news.

"I miss hearing his typewriter," Judy told her father, who was there when Lorraine came in.

"Is it all right?" she asked, peeping through the half-open door. "The nurse at the desk downstairs said I could come up for a little while."

"Of course it's all right. You two girls may have the room to yourselves," Dr. Bolton told them. "I'm on my way out. I'll see you at home, Judy girl."

"Did he sign you out?" asked Lorraine when he was gone. "That's wonderful, Judy! I guess you won't be needing these."

The room was filled with flowers. Judy added the bouquet Lorraine gave her to the collection. "I'll take them all home. People have been so good to me."

"I haven't," Lorraine said. "I didn't mean to upset you the other day, but I've been so mixed up. You solved everything else. That man will go to prison—"

"Not Dick? They aren't going to send him back. Peter talked with his parole officer. He understands how it was."

"Arthur doesn't," Lorraine said with a deep sigh. "He thinks I should have suspected those signatures were forged. I could have written to the Brandts."

"Peter did get in touch with them," Judy told her. "They didn't lease their estate. They left Stanley to take care of it, and he allowed the gang to move in. Falco must have bribed him or something. I think the Brandts hired Roger Banning, too. He was supposed to repair the fountain."

"It wasn't repaired when we were there," Lorraine remembered.

"I know. Roger was forced to work for the gang, instead. They made him bring his friend along. Dick didn't know what they were up to at first, but when he found out it was extortion he refused to have any part of it. He told Horace all about it."

Judy had seen the papers and read her brother's story, but there were still a few pieces of the puzzle that didn't fit.

"The police didn't find the jewels they were looking for," she continued. "I told Peter they should
have looked in the fountain. Lorraine, there is a locked
room down under it. The loot from their robberies
might be stored there. Peter knows about it now. He'll
get back your ring."

"I hope he will. Lois said there wasn't anything
you couldn't solve," Lorraine remembered, "and I
guess that goes for Peter, too. Everybody else knew
I was doing wrong before I did. I don't expect
Arthur to forgive me, but if we had the ring back
he might unbend a little and stop being so cold and
polite all the time."

"He's that way because he's hurt," Judy explained.
"Most men are like that. Girls cry, but men just
hold it all in and hurt back, or else they get angry
and shout. I think Peter would get angry."

"I wish Arthur would get angry! I deserve it after
all the trouble I've caused."

"Lorraine," Judy said, taking her hand, "did it ever
occur to you that you felt exactly the way Falco
intended you to feel? Peter says that's the way confidence men work, and Falco was a confidence man
as well as a jewel thief and an extortioner. Roger
Banning, the Cubberlings, and Dick Hartwell were
all victims of his vicious lies. He should be behind
bars for a long, long time."

"I guess he will be, but that doesn't solve my

problem. I don't think there is a solution," Lorraine declared. "Arthur knows I deceived him. I told him I went to the movies with you the night I met Falco. I even said I was calling from the movies when I was actually calling from the Brandt place. He and Peter had arranged to trace the call. They knew it wasn't true. Now Arthur will never trust me."

"Do you trust him? I mean completely?" asked Judy. "Before this happened, weren't there a few little doubts in your mind? Weren't you afraid to let him have friends for fear he'd like them better than you? Be honest with yourself, Lorraine, and be honest with him, and I think everything will work out in time."

"I hope it will," Lorraine replied, as she rose to leave.

"You might trust the rest of us a little bit, too, while you're at it," Judy added. "Just keep on believing the stolen jewels will be found and we'll keep on trying to find them. Peter hasn't given up yet, you know. And pretty soon I'll be well enough to help him."

"It isn't just the ring," Lorraine said, "but it would help if I had it. 'Bye, Judy, and thanks—for everything."

CHAPTER XXIV

The Secret of the Fountain

JUDY was home at last. The cast would soon be removed from her foot and she would be ready for the next exciting chapter in a life that had, so far, been a series of problems and solutions.

Blackberry was curled contentedly in Judy's lap unconscious of the fact that the collar he wore was now decorated with a life-saving medal.

"A cat is good publicity," the editor, Mr. Lee, had told Horace. "The public gets tired of dog stories. But a cat—well, that's different. When a cat saves a life that's really news."

The life he was talking about was the life of Dick Hartwell. "In another five minutes," Dr. Bolton was telling the group in the living room, "it would have

173

been too late to save him. I didn't know you were in the tower, Judy girl, when I hurried past—"

"I'm glad you hurried, Dad," she told him. "If you'd stopped to help me, Dick would have died, wouldn't he? I can see why you told Falco he was dead, but why did you say Horace was dead, too? I've been meaning to ask you. It was the end of the world for me when I heard it. I tease him and torment him, and we've often quarreled with each other. *Anything you can do I can do better*, that sort of stuff. But I really love my brother."

"I know you do, Judy girl. I really love that son of mine, too," Dr. Bolton said. "That's why I hurried him out of there so fast. 'Neither of them will do much talking,' I told that gangster and the woman who was with him. Then I covered the boys' faces and we rushed them to the ambulance, where a pulmotor was waiting to revive them. Peter was there by then. The police, Dick's parole officer, and several more Federal agents came soon afterwards. But I was alone at first. It was a ticklish situation."

"I see. I guess you did what you had to do, the same as I did."

"That's right. Maybe you learned your strategy from your old dad. You know how strict I am about the truth. Don't misunderstand me," the doctor warned. "I wouldn't stretch it even a little way unless there was a life at stake. It wasn't far from the truth, anyway. Horace was unconscious—"

"He doesn't look it now!"

Judy was through being serious. Her brother was at the table devouring a huge piece of cake that Honey had just cut for him. Peter had a slice nearly as large. The house was full of people as it had been ever since Judy came home. Lois, Lorraine, and Arthur were there. Other friends and neighbors were in and out, glad of a chance to help Judy, although she insisted she was well able to help herself. She could walk with the cast on her foot, but not very gracefully. Everybody had autographed it, even Blackberry with his paw print. The next guest to arrive was Helen Brandt, home early from what had started out to be a winter vacation.

"We came right home as soon as we got Peter's message," she explained. "Imagine Stanley letting those criminals move in, and then saying, 'Every man has his price.' I don't believe it, do you, Judy?"

"No, I don't," she said. "Peter, come here and meet Helen Brandt. She'll be interested in hearing about that cache of jewels you found down under the fountain."

"So that's the secret you two have been keeping!" several of Judy's friends exclaimed.

"I can't believe it!" cried Helen. "That used to be a storeroom. There was an outside door then—"

"They walled it in and stuffed the loot from dozens

of robberies between the wall and the door. It was concealed from the inside, too, but not quite well enough. The only entrance they left clear was the one under the cupids. If they hadn't dropped one of their stolen diamonds by accident on the way in, we might have given up the search. Judy found it," Peter finished proudly.

"I pretended it was a frozen tear. Can you guess why, Helen?" asked Judy. "Were you there, the day, years ago, when I came with my grandparents?"

"I remember," Helen Brandt replied. She was a little vague about it, but soon her explanation of the unsolved mystery began to make sense. "Your grandmother said she'd found you crying over the picture of our fountain," she told Judy. "The picture appeared once in a magazine with an article about gardens. I guess your grandmother had the magazine. You know it's an old fountain, don't you? It's been there ever since my mother can remember."

"Tell us about the rooms under it. I'd like to see them," declared Honey.

"They were built underground so we could have heat down there in the winter to keep the pipes from freezing. The caretaker we had before Stanley used to live down there and take care of the pipes. He suggested making the other room into a playroom for me," Helen continued, "but he died before it was finished. I used to pretend things about his ghost."

Judy shivered. "I didn't need to pretend things. The moans we heard were real."

"It was Dick Hartwell," Lois whispered. "They had him locked up in one of those rooms."

"What was in the other one?"

This question was ignored as Helen Brandt went on with her story. "Stanley wouldn't fix anything. The fountain used to be pretty. We wanted it that way again, so we hired Mr. Banning. He's a plumber, you know. He sent his son, Roger, to do the work—"

"That fits," agreed Peter.

"But what about that other voice Judy heard?" asked Horace. "We still haven't figured out that one."

"I think I have," Judy told him. "Helen, if you heard what my grandparents were saying, and then found me crying again, you must have pretended you were the fountain."

"You used to be full of tricks, Helen," Lois put in. "When we played dolls together you were always talking for them and pretending they came to life at midnight—things like that."

Honey laughed. "That must be how it happened, Judy. Now I won't be afraid to go down there. That is, if I'm ever invited."

"You pretended a lot of other things, didn't you, Helen?" asked Judy. "I mean things like wishes that came true if you shed a tear in the fountain."

"I read about it in a fairy story once," Helen

Brandt confessed. "There were two sisters. The good one shed tears that turned into diamonds, but the tears the other one shed changed into toads. I tried it on you just for fun. Then I peeked out from behind those cupids and watched you wish. But what were you crying about? Your tears looked real."

"They were," declared Judy. "Growing up isn't easy. There are lots of things to cry about when you're fourteen."

"I know," Helen said. "When you've outgrown your dolls and you're not old enough for boys—"

"Didn't you have any pets, Judy?"

Judy wasn't sure who asked the question. She held up Blackberry for inspection. "I wasn't very old when I got him," she said. "He was such an adorable kitten. But now he's old and wise and decorated with medals. If I had another wish to make in the fountain, do you know what it would be?"

Everybody gathered around Judy to hear.

"I'd wish that Blackberry would never grow old and die," she told them. "I'd wish he could live forever and ever. If your fountain can make a wish like that come true, I'll stop thinking it's haunted."

"But Judy," Lois objected. "Nothing could make an impossible wish like that come true."

"Oh, I don't know," Lorraine said with a meaning glance in Arthur's direction. "Sometimes Judy manages to do the impossible. She found the diamond that started all this and led to the discovery of that walled-in hiding place—and my ruby. It means more now than it ever did. Arthur will tell you. We talked it all over, and now he really understands."

Judy could see it was true. Arthur smiled at Lorraine in the old, devoted way. And Horace and Honey were more devoted than ever in spite of her art work.

"The fountain inspired me," Honey declared. "I designed a new fabric. It has little fountains all over it. The air brush makes beautiful spray. Judy, you'll love to have a dress made out of it."

"Could I have one, too?" asked Helen Brandt. "You wouldn't mind if I had a dress like yours, would you, Judy? I mean if I told you how your wish about Blackberry could come true."

"You're joking," Judy said. "No cat can live forever."

"Cats have kittens," Helen pointed out. "Blackberry didn't come to our house because of the fish we have there. He was paying a social call. I have a cat, too. Her name is Tabby and if she has kittens—"

"Promise me," Judy interrupted, "that if one of them looks like Blackberry you will give it to me. I'd like my little namesake, Judy Meredith, to have a black kitten and name it Blackberry, too. Did I tell you we've been invited to spend Christmas with Dale and Irene in New York? They're little Judy's parents," Judy explained to Helen Brandt. All the rest of them knew Irene's Cinderella story. "Isn't it wonderful?"

Everybody thought so except Judy's young neighbor, Holly Potter.

"We traded birthdays. Remember? You were going to have yours on Christmas so I could have mine last September when we opened the forbidden chest."

"That's right," the others agreed. "You two girls did trade birthdays."

Helen Brandt had an idea.

"Why not have the celebration just before Judy and Peter leave for New York? We can have it in that room under the fountain. We'll open it up and make a playroom and set up a Christmas tree."

"Not there," Judy objected. "I'd love to have a party at your house, Helen, and make another wish in the fountain. I'll think of how I felt when I thought Horace was drowned, and the tears will come easy. But please, not in the tunnel. There are real ghosts down there. The fountain will always be haunted—"

"Objection!" shouted Peter. "Enchanted is the word you want. I ask but one favor. Promise me, Angel, that when you make your next wish I'll be there to grant it."

"You will have to be." Judy's gray eyes were tender. "Because my wish will be that you'll always be there."

Printed in the United States
119140LV00003B/271-297/P